ANDALUC__

MYSTERIES

A COLLECTION OF SHORT STORIES

By John Hardy

TABLE OF CONTENTS

ACKNOWLEDGEMENTS

I would like to dedicate this book to Wendy, without whose help and encouragement it would not have been produced. Not to mention her typing of the work and her mastering of Word to get it into the right format. In her conquest of computer skills, we would both wish to credit the help given by Don and Jane.

I would also like to thank Paco, painter and decorator, saxophone player but above all photographer and friend, and Adele his partner, for the photo of Sedella on the front cover.

Lastly I must thank "la gente de mi pueblo", the people of my village, who have made Wendy and I welcome.

PREFACE

A collection of 12 short stories of crime, mystery and suspense set on the Costa del Sol, some with a humorous touch, and all with a twist in the tail. The stories involve British ex-pats and holiday makers living or staying on the coast, many of them involving their relationships with the local community.

All the stories are set in actual situations, though some of them use fictitious names of villages, rather than their real ones. As an example of this, the bank and village described in "Bank Robbery" actually exists as portrayed in the story, however the name and location of the village are fictional. Many of the events used in the stories are also based on actual incidents, some of which happened to, or were witnessed by myself, but once again the stories no relation to the factual occasion. An example of this is the bar in "The Vine", where a local English resident was always given, as a wind-up by the barman, hot milk with her tea, not cold as she wanted.

THE VINE

It was mid afternoon and the man was sitting outside a bar in the hot September sun, somewhere in what he had discovered on his map to be the Axarquía in southern Spain. From where he sat, just to the side of the door, he could see over his right shoulder the barman, alone now in the empty bar, busily catching up washing glasses after what must have been a busy lunchtime trade. As he looked inside the barman caught sight of his glance and smiled, raising his shoulders. "Mucho trabajo, poco dinero," he called out. Not understanding a word, but unwilling to show his ignorance, the man grinned back. "Er, yes," he replied and then quickly corrected himself, "Si, si, OK, yes." It was no good, he thought, he must concentrate on the phrase book he had bought only two days ago at Gatwick airport. He turned his glance away from the bar and looked down at the novel he was trying to read. That was no good either, he thought, why hadn't he bought some books to read as well as the Spanish/English phrase book at the airport? He had picked this one at random from his bookcase just before leaving home. It was one left over from his childhood, Dickens' "Tale of Two Cities". Listlessly he tried to concentrate once more on its contents but his mind would not focus on it at all.

"It was the best of times, it was the worst of times," he thought morosely. No, it was only the worst of times. What was he doing here anyway? He never went on holidays, never, and if he took time off at all, he spent it watching cricket or football or decorating, either that or watching the telly, he added honestly. It was all Jennifer's fault, she, his sister, had insisted. "Get away, get some sun, relax," she had gone on and on until he had agreed, just for a bit of peace. She had done all the arranging, booked his flight, and his hire car, bought him some pesetas and waved him off. "See you in two weeks, enjoy yourself," she had called out as he went through the barrier at the airport. Enjoy yourself, he thought, gazing unseeing at the page in front of him, as if. But he was tired, he needed rest he mentally agreed, he was drained after a damaging six months.

He took stock, he was 34 and a successful Detective Inspector with the Eastshire force. A rising talent! That was part of the trouble, he was totally immersed in his work, one reason why he did not, and had not for years, taken a holiday. He had not even taken his full quota of leave, he admitted to himself. It was time to be honest, to face up to things,that was what this holiday was supposed to be about, that and having a break. Just a few months ago Jill, his wife, had walked out demanding a divorce. "You're never here," she had complained. "Always working, we never go anywhere, do anything together. Thank God we've no kids. So that's it, Andrew, I'm off. It's not too late for me, I'm only 30 and young enough to make a fresh start."

He had been stunned and unable to reply, or even, he admitted now from the safety of both time and place, to take it all in. He had just started a new case, a devastating dreadful and time consuming case, of child abuse and murder. He was fully consumed and psychologically numbed by it, and focussed on solving it to the exclusion of everything else, his own situation included. So Jill had disappeared from his life almost without his awareness, on the surface at least. And then just two weeks ago the case was solved, but the suspect, knowing he had been discovered, had killed himself rather messily, and he blamed himself for that too, because he had not, by his own reasoning, moved fast enough.

"Look Andrew, you can't take everything on to yourself," his Superintendent had said. "You're drained, the case, a nasty one, your divorce, Elliot's suicide. Go on leave, that's an order, you're due God knows how much time off, and you're no good to us in this state. Go away! Come back when you've sorted things out a bit. Got them in balance."

And so here he was, in the sun, sipping on ice-cold beer, outside a bar in God knows where, trying to read a book he had once found enjoyable but could not now be bothered with . . . .

His deepening gloom and self pity was interrupted by voices, English ones. Two women were coming down the steps leading from the road on to the terrace. Middle aged, engrossed in a conversation.

"I thought we'd stop here for a drink before we go on, it's not far now, and then you can have a lay down after your journey. I don't know about you, but I'm parched." The speaker was dressed casually in a cotton dress and sunhat, black hair showing under it. Her companion was more formally attired, and sweating in a two piece suit. They entered the bar, and the one who obviously lived locally said, "Tea alright, Dot?' Dos té, Paco, con leche," this last to the barman. "We'll have leche, sorry milk, Dot, is that alright? He does a good tea here, in a pot, not in the cups."

The barman turned to his gleaming coffee machine behind him, put two teabags into a stainless steel pot and filled it with hot water, that came hissing and steaming out of the pipe. Then he took a small metal jug and filled it with milk, and putting it under the same spout, proceeded to steam-heat it.

"Cold milk, Paco, cold, oh! bother the man. Frio, frio, leche FRIO," she was almost shouting. She turned to her companion, "He always does this to me, he should know by now I always have cold milk."

The barman paused and turned to face her. "Frio, leche frio?" he asked with raised eyebrows and exaggerated surprise. "Frio, no caliente?" "No, not hot, no caliente," replied the woman crossly. The barman caught sight of Andrew looking at him from over his shoulder, and his eyes sparkled briefly, a half smile forming about his lips. He's sending her up, Andrew thought, he obviously always does it, he smiled back as the barman poured out a second jug of, this time, cold milk.

Andrew went back to his book, but something was buzzing in the back of his mind, he knew the woman. Don't be silly, he told himself, but the thought persisted. Something about her, the way she had reacted, her anger, her voice. His mind, used to worrying at problems, would not let it go. The women were leaving, he looked at his watch amazed, fifteen minutes had passed, then as they passed him and she looked sideways at him, he had it. Jane Hobson, wife of Alfie, who he had met after Alfie had escaped from prison, about ten years ago. Alf Hobson was in prison for a bank robbery, but had been found not guilty of the murder of a bank clerk during the robbery. Then he had escaped, never to be found, and no money had been recovered. Andrew had been only 24 and a new Detective Constable when he had gone to check out Alfie's wife, Jane, to see if there was any sign of the wanted man. He remembered her defiance at the time, her anger. "He won't come anywhere near me," she'd shouted at him. "Go away and leave me alone, I've done nothing wrong."

Even as he was thinking, Andrew had risen, paid for the beer and started up the steps after the two women. What should he do? Jane Hobson had vanished about a year later when the surveillance on her had had to be reduced. What should he do? he asked himself again. He was on holiday, in a strange land, he had no authority here, did not even know the law. But two million pounds was still missing, as well as Alfie. He saw the two women reach a car parked down the road and get in. He got into his own car, fortunately facing the same way, and pulled out after them. He must at least find out where they were going, where Jane lived, and Alfie too? He wondered.

The car in front led him through the small village of Tejedos, near the bar, and out the other side. About two kilometres or so after that it turned into an entrance to a villa. The villa was enclosed inside a high hedge. He drove past the entrance and pulled off the road some way past. Locking the car, he walked back to the gateway and looked cautiously in at the house. Jane's car was parked on some gravel in front of the house, but there was no sign of life at all. He walked back to the corner of the garden, and made his way along the edge of a vineyard until he found a small gap in the hedge and looked through. He was looking at a terrace with a swimming pool at the back of the villa. In the water was a girl with long black hair. Jane Hobson came out of the back door, calling out over her shoulder, "Just put your things in the room, Dot, and then have a lie down, a siesta. Hi Molly," she called to the girl in the water, "Aunt Dot's here, go in and say hello before she dozes off."

Molly Hobson, Andrew thought, watching as the girl came out of the pool, water cascading off her attractive body. She was only a frightened ten year old the last time he had seen her, large dark eyes fearfully peering at him from a thin face, with an awkward skinny body. A bit different now, he mused, looking at her shapely form in a miniscule bikini. She disappeared into the house, returning a few minutes later in a pair of shorts and a brightly coloured top. "I'm just going into Tejedos to see Maria, mum, Aunt Dot's fine, nearly asleep. See you in a bit," and she was gone. The harsh rattle of a moped started at the front of the house, and then went off down the road and quiet descended on the scene. What now, he thought.

He made his way back to the corner of the field, along the road to the gate and walked up the drive. He went down the side of the villa and cautiously looked across the terrace to where the woman sat, a jug of orange juice beside her on the table.

"Come in," she called quietly, startling him, "Constable Farthing isn't it? Or is it Sergeant now?" "Inspector, actually," he managed as he advanced. Trust Jane, he thought, everyone always said she was a quick thinker, and intelligent. How she had got mixed up with the likes of Alfie Hobson was always a mystery to the whole team who had been on the case. He had been violent to her as well, he recalled, a vicious thug, suspected of at least two murders and numerous assaults.

"Congratulations, Inspector hey? You were a bit wet behind the ears when we met," she said. "Are you here officially?"

"No, I'm just on holiday, but I recognised you at the bar. How did you know I was here?"

"I recognised you too, as we were leaving," she answered. "Though you've filled out a bit. And you shouldn't wear a white shirt if you want to hide, I could see it through the hedge. I saw you get into your car and follow me too. Now not too much noise, as my sister's asleep. If you're looking for Alf, he's not here, I haven't seen him for years. Sit down and have a glass of orange."

He saw that a second glass had been placed ready for him on the table, she was obviously a clever lady.

"Thanks," he sat down. "You must realise I've no standing here, but I have a duty to find your husband." There was ice in the orange, which was freshly squeezed, and it was pleasant on the terrace, and cool in the shade of a large vine that grew in the corner and spread out over the whole area.

"I'll be honest with you," she began, "I did follow Alfie out here, he sent for me when things cooled off. I was never married to him, ah I see you didn't know that, someone slipped up there." Superintendent Dodds, Andrew thought, just about to retire and one of the old school, bang a confession out of somebody, and don't bother with too much clever stuff. But someone should have looked into her background. She was going on, "Well, I had a passport in my own name. That's Johnson, so I'm Jane Johnson, or Juana as they call me here now. Alf bought himself a new passport in the same name after he escaped, he had enough money to buy himself what he wanted," she added bitterly. "He'd also bought this place and was well settled by the time I arrived. But the locals didn't like him, well it was hard to like Alf. So Molly and me, we settled down too, but things were never good. He'd always hit me of course." She paused. Looking at her Andrew thought, she's tough, no sign now of a battered wife, as there had been at their first meeting. "He'd always hit me," she took up the story again, "but I could cope, then one day he hit Molly. She was only thirteen, going on fourteen, we'd been here about a year then and she was well in with the local kids. She went to school here, well one night they all

12

went to some disco or other, and she got back late. He couldn't abide being defied, and he'd told her to be back by midnight, well it was two in the morning when she got back, things tend to go on late here you know. There was no harm in it, she was with a group, and you don't get problems here like in England." She paused again, gazing into the distance, then continued again. "That was it as far as I was concerned, I told him, me yes, her no. I made him go away for good."

Andrew sat there thinking, was it true? Should he just leave it? But how had she 'made him go away for good?' Had she threatened to split on him, contact the police, tell them who he was? And what about the money? That was still missing. Even if she really didn't know where Alf was, she might know about that.

"You really have no idea where he is, he really went away and you've not heard from him since?" he asked, playing for time. She was silent for a long time, dreamily looking up into the leaves of the vine over their heads. At last she broke the silence, cutting into his thoughts. "Antonio, an old man in the village, just after I arrived here when I was planning this terrace, told me that if I wanted to grow a big healthy vine, I should do what the locals used to do at one time. He said they would bury a donkey beneath the plant, and that it would feed on it for years."

The sound of the moped entering the gate came to them, followed by rapid steps down the side of the house, and Molly appeared at the corner. "Hi mum, oh hello, who are you?"

"This is an old friend," replied Jane. "He just turned up unexpectedly, he's on holiday and........ well, looked me up. Andrew, meet Molly, my daughter, Molly meet Andrew. Now, Molly, Aunt Dot and I are going into the village to eat tonight, will you come with us as well, or have you other plans?" Molly was eyeing Andrew with a certain look in her eyes. He's not bad, she thought, and presumably on his own. He sensed her interest and was smitten in return. He felt fresh and alive for the first time in months. If Alf really had gone, he decided he would do nothing to disturb the life of either Molly or her mother. To hell with the money, but he must make sure Alf was not still here.

Molly kept her eyes on him as she answered her mother with a look of what? promise? challenge? "Sure, I'll come with you, and you'll join us Andrew, won't you? Then I'll have someone to talk to when Mum and Aunt Dot talk family together."

"Well, er, I'm not sure . . . .," he trailed off, wanting to say yes, but knowing he couldn't intrude in this family, him of all people. Yet he had not felt so carefree, so refreshed, for years. This was the cure he needed, but . . . . "Yes, do, Andrew," said Jane, smiling at him. "Great, that's settled," said Molly. "I'm going for a shower, see you in a while."

Jane reached above her head and picked a bunch of grapes. "What was I saying, yes, well, I was finished with Alfie when he hit Molly, you can imagine, she's everything to me. He was a violent man you know, always beating up someone, and he had killed three people to my knowledge. Violent and vicious he was, I don't know how I ever got involved with him. Well I do, but I was younger then, and wild myself. Oh well, as I said, that was the end, hitting Molly like that." She broke a grape off, and put it into her mouth, handing another to Andrew. "Have a grape, they're so juicy, Antonio says he's never seen such a strong healthy plant as this vine. I said to him, Antonio, when I planted it, that I didn't have a donkey to bury under it." She paused again and ate another grape. Andrew felt a chill   settle over him, despite the heat of the early evening, cold shivers running up his spine.

"You asked about Alf, yes, he's gone for good. What did everyone call him? An ox of a man, that's right, and he was stubborn, oh he was stubborn. Stubborn as a . . . . as a mule, isn't it?" Andrew felt himself relax, with a light heart he followed Jane across the terrace and into the house. "I'll just get my car," he said, "then if I could, I'll have a shower and change before we go to eat."

Outside, on the empty terrace, the vine cast its cooling shade.

CAVEAT EMPTOR

"Did you have a good holiday?"

"What?" I looked up from my paper in annoyance and turned to the man in the next seat.

"Sorry, didn't you hear me? Noise of the engines I expect. I only asked if you had had a good holiday."

The plane from Málaga to Gatwick had just taken off and was banking steeply over the sea, turning to head back over the city and on to its destination. In the departure lounge, on the short bus ride from the departure gate to the plane, and after sitting in my seat, I had avoided contact with the other passengers. Since then I had been quietly reading my newspaper, not wanting to join in a conversation with strangers.

"Actually I'm going on holiday, not coming back, I live in Spain," I said, turning back to my paper and hoping he would take the hint and stop disturbing me.

"Do you?" he persisted. "That's interesting, I'm in the process of trying to buy out here too. No luck this time though."

"Right," I responded, without looking up. A discreet noise sounded over the loudspeakers and the seat belt sign went off. We were informed about the height at which we would be flying, the speed of the plane, its arrival time in London and advised to keep our seat belts fastened for our own safety, first in Spanish and then in English. Taking advantage of the hiatus in my reading as I waited for the announcement to finish, my neighbour went on to tell me that he had spent the previous week touring the area "from Mojácar to La Linea", looking for property. He had visited several estate agents, "on the spur of the moment, you know, no appointments, just turned up at their offices". This was, he assured me, the best way, they had no time to "dream up scams". He hadn't however had any luck.

I kept my eyes on the page, hoping in vain he'd get the message, hearing his voice drone on next to me, some bits piercing my thoughts, other bits just a background noise. "I'd had no trouble with any of them, except one. A real cowboy he was, tried all sorts of fast ones on me. Tall man, black spade-like beard and long black hair. Well spoken type, now what was his name?"

"Jack Pendlebury," I thought, my attention caught at last.

"Jack something or other, Penter ..... Peddler .... Pen...

"Pendlebury," I said, lowering my paper.

"That's right, Jack Pendlebury. Do you know him? Not a friend or anything, I hope."

"No. Not a friend. Met him once," I answered.

All around us, suddenly, there was a surge of movement. Tables being lowered, meal trays handed out. During this break in our conversation, I looked out of the window and gazed down through the thin white streaks of cloud at the brown barren land of central Iberia. Here and there darker patches of land patterned the landscape, whilst in the distance a line of sierras was visible. Yes, I had met Jack Pendlebury once, and it had stuck in my memory ever since. It must have been over twelve years ago, when I too was house hunting, but the event was as clear as if it were yesterday.

I had sent the outline of what I was looking for to his agency the week before my visit, so that he could sort out suitable sites to look at. That way we would not waste each other's time. "Somewhere in the campo, not in a town or village. Some way inland, say six or so miles minimum, with plenty of land. I don't care if there's a building or not, or what state it's in. I can build or refurbish as necessary. The site is what's important." That or something like it is what I'd told him in the letter. I'd turned up at his office at 10am as arranged and, fortunately as it turned out, decided to follow him in my hire car, rather than go in his, so that I could move on from wherever we ended up. He'd taken me out of the town, Mojácar, and driven off inland. We'd passed under the N340 motorway and then gone on into the dry, brown, dusty hinterland before turning off the small country road on to a dirt track. About 500 metres down the track he'd pulled up next to an electricity pylon, and we'd both got out. He was standing at the edge of a small "valley", looking down into it. The "valley" was about 400 metres across and about 15 metres deep, with a flat wide base.

"That's where you'll be able to get your power," he'd said, pointing at the pylon. "And there's a water main under the track. The site stretches from this side of the valley to the other and about a kilometre of its length." He paused and pointed down into the "valley". "That's where you'll build your house, on the level bit at the bottom."

I'd looked at him. I didn't know much about Spain then, but I did know there had been a drought for a few years, and I could tell a dry river bed from a "valley". When the rains came, and come they would, any house built down there wouldn't last five minutes.

"Thanks a lot," I'd said. "Goodbye," and without any more ado I'd got back into my car and driven off.

"Wait," his voice had followed me. "If you don't like it, I've more . . . ."

"This looks good, doesn't it," my fellow passenger's voice brought me back to the present. I looked down at my tray. On it

18

was a small salad, a bread bun, some meat and veg, and what looked like a peach sponge or some suchlike.

"Uh. Well, so so," I managed. "Vino tinto," I added to the stewardess who had just put the tray in front of me. All around people were taking off plastic wrapping and starting to eat. I broke the seal on my wine and poured some into my plastic glass before the tackling the salad.

"He was a right cowboy, that Pendlebury, don't know how well you know him, but he really tried to do me. But nobody does that to me and gets away with it."

"Right," I said, at a loss for words. "I don't really know him, just met him the once, house hunting you know."

I looked more directly at my fellow_passenger. He was a big raw-looking man with strong heavy arms, on one of which I could see a tattoo of a snake. He looked strong and tough and there was an angry glint in his eyes.

"Told him I wanted a place, just outside the town, enough land for a pool. That sort of thing. First he took me to a place in the town, no room to swing a cat. Then out into the country to an old villa, nearly falling down, right next to a pig farm. Then another with no track to it, and then one with no room for a fish pond never mind a swimming pool. A whole day he wasted, my first one it was, just over a week ago, and I had to get to Marbella the next day to look round there. Nothing he showed me was anything like what I wanted. And some of the problems weren't obvious, I had to work them out for myself."

"Caveat emptor," I murmured.

"What?"

"Buyer beware."

"Oh. Right. Yeah. He tried all sorts of things, good job I'd my wits about me. But the last one really got my goat. Sent me over the top I can tell you."

Again there was a welcome break as the trays were gathered up. Once more I looked out of the window, but all I could see was cloud, rolling away in all directions.

"Do you know what he tried next?" His voice once more cut into my thoughts that had gone, reluctantly, back to the purpose of my visit to England. My sister had left her husband, or rather he had left her, and she had begged me to come back and help her sort things out.

"You'll have to go," my wife had insisted. "Just for a week. Help her with finances, the house, the children, all that sort of thing." So with a heavy heart, I'd taken the first available flight.

I shook my head. "No, what did he try?"

"We were looking round this finca place. Just right in many ways. Fair size, quite good nick, a fair bit of land, and only about a mile or so out of Mojácar. He says to me that it would take a bit of renovating but that there was power and water. He pointed to a pipe that came through the wall with a tap on. "It'll need plumbing of course," he said. I tried the tap but nothing came out. "Oh, it's turned off," he said to me, "but the town hall will soon turn it on again when you pay the water rates."

He paused, looking at me in a grim way.

"What then?" I asked. "What was the problem?"

He nodded at me with a small smile on his lips, that didn't reach his eyes. "Later on, I walked round the house, looking at the land, and do you know what I noticed?"

"No." I couldn't imagine, but I didn't like the look on his face.

20

"I saw the end of a pipe. There was no water, that pipe was just poked through the wall. Not connected to anything. I lost my temper with him then."

During the silence that followed, the pilot's voice came over the speakers to tell us that we would be landing in a short time at Gatwick, to fasten our seat belts, that the temperature in London was twelve degrees, that it was raining, and that he hoped that we would fly with them again I looked out of the window and saw green fields with a road winding through them, over in the distance was a lake and nearer a village. Soon we would be landing where I would be met by my sister and be plunged into her chaos and misery. I glanced again at my paper and folded it away. My neighbour had now finally stopped talking and lapsed into a moody silence.

The last I saw of him he was striding away from baggage control with his luggage which had been one of the first off the belt, whilst mine as usual was obviously going to be the last. As I stood waiting I opened my paper again, it was that day's copy of "Sur in English" and, because of the interruptions of my fellow passenger, I'd not got past the first page. Now I looked inside and read the main headline on the second page.

"Mysterious death of English Estate Agent". Pushing my trolley of cases, I read on. Apparently an English estate agent, Jack Pendlebury, had been found battered to death at a remote deserted finca near Mojácar the previous week. No one knew what he was doing there, or who if anyone he'd been showing around. "It's been on our books for ages," his assistant was quoted as saying, "but it's in a poor state, and has no water, we just couldn't sell it."

I went through the barrier in a turmoil of thought. What should I do? Who was the man who had sat next to me and was he anything to do with it? Or had the agent taken someone else to view the house? Or was his death connected to something else altogether?

Suddenly my thoughts were interrupted by my sister, shaking me by the arm. "Where are you going, didn't you see me? Oh, I don't know what I'm going to do . . . ."

Later in the car, still being deluged by her woes, I realised I'd dropped or mislaid the paper. At least it was no longer in my possession.

What should I do, what would you do?

"And then there's the bank account to sort out, it's a joint one, and the insurance policies, and where am I going to live? He wants to sell the house. Are you listening to me at all?"

What can I do?

SISTERS

Roger still came to stay with me several times even after the death of Kate, his wife and my sister. Bill, my husband, and I were both very fond of his two girls, who we treated almost as our own. Even after the sudden death of Bill, whilst he was in England on business, the three of them visited me as usual. This year however, with both girls away at college, I was surprised when Roger rang to say he'd like to come as usual during the spring half term. I'd agreed of course and so here we were sitting on the terrace, with Roger mixing gin and tonics at the small bar Bill had built just inside the living room door.

All I could see of him was his back, busily moving from side to side as he opened the bottles and poured out the drinks. I glanced idly at the mirror on the opposite wall and saw him tip something from a small bottle into one of the glasses. This puzzled me, but then I thought, perhaps he's on medication or something and doesn't want to tell me. He came back on to the terrace and placed one glass in front of me and the other by his side on the small table that was between us. It can't be medication, I thought in some confusion, not put into alcohol.

"Do you like my new picture I bought in Fuengirola last week?" I asked, pointing back into the lounge. He turned to look over his shoulder at the oil painting by a local artist of Málaga harbour. "It's very good, was it very expensive?" he said, turning back.

Just like him to think of the cost, I thought. "No, not very, well, cheers." I picked up my drink and sipped it.

"Cheers, bottoms up," and he downed his drink at one go and got up to replenish his glass. When he came back, I finished mine too and rose.

"No, don't get up, I'll do it myself," I told him as he started to rise and went and mixed myself another.

I'm not describing this very clearly, am I, perhaps I'd better start at the beginning. Kate and I grew up in Ilford in Essex, and we met Roger and Bill at a disco in Leyton about twenty five years ago. Roger and Bill were long standing friends and the four of us paired off. Eventually we got married and over the next few years were always close to each other. Bill's father had a small factory in Grays and eventually Bill took it over and built it up, then opened two more and we became relatively rich.

Roger was a biology teacher at a comprehensive in Stratford and they were not anything like so well off. We might have become less close if it wasn't for the two girls. Bill and I discovered quite early on in our marriage that we couldn't have children, whilst Kate and Roger soon had two lovely young girls. Both Bill and I love children, and as uncle and aunt as well as godparents to them both, became very attached to them and we visited each others houses frequently.

When the girls were six and seven respectively, Bill had a mild heart attack and was told to slow down. What we finally decided to do was to buy a villa out here in Spain where he could relax and run his factories using short visits to England, the telephone and fax, and recently the internet. He had very good managers in all his factories, which now number five in all.

Roger, Kate and the girls visited us every school holiday with us often paying the fares, as Roger's salary could not stretch that far.

We were pleased to do this as over the years the girls had become almost like daughters to us. As we had no children of our own and Bill was an only child, and I had no other family but Kate, we even drew up our wills in favour of the girls, or rather in favour of Kate who would, by agreement between her and myself, use it for their education and then when they were twenty one pass it over to them. Kate and I had always been close and I knew I could trust her fully in this. When the girls reached twenty one then, we were all agreed, we would draw up new wills in their favour. In the event of Kate's death before this time, we put in a clause naming Roger in her place. You may think it strange that we only put Kate's name on the will, and Roger's only if she died, but to tell you the truth I've never really trusted him. I've always felt he begrudged Bill his business success and envied him too much. He's always going on about the cost of things, like my picture for instance, and how little they have. It used to embarrass my sister, I know. Anyway, Bill didn't want his name on the will either, despite their long friendship, and so Kate alone was named.

Our villa is out past Coin in the Sierra de Canucha, and so was handy for the airport, the beach, the towns of Marbella, Fuengirola, Torremolinos and Málaga. It is also easy to get to Ronda and the lakes near Ardales, both places the girls adored visiting.

This was the way things were until two years ago when Kate contracted cancer, and was dead in less than twelve months. As I've said already, Roger and the girls still came out a few times together after that, and Bill and I were glad to have them come. In fact we insisted they did, for they needed to get away for a break, and we wanted to see the girls. Bill and I did nothing about the will, it's not something we really thought about in any case.

Then just two months ago Bill went to England to do his twice yearly tour of his factories. I'll never forget the day the two Guardia came to my door, one male and one female, to tell me he'd been killed. They were very kind and sympathetic, but I just couldn't believe it. He'd apparently fallen under a tube train in the rush hour at Holborn station. It was an accident of course, no thought that he'd done it deliberately, the platform was crowded and those nearest said he'd apparently stumbled under pressure from behind him.

When I got over the first shock I wrote to the girls, who were now both at University, and told them I was looking forward to seeing them in the summer holidays. I also told them that I meant to change my will to make them direct beneficiaries now, and not when they were twenty one. They knew all about the conditions in the old will, we made sure of that once they were in their early teens. I didn't write to tell Roger of my intentions and didn't know if either of them had mentioned it to him.

And then, just a week ago, Roger had rung to say he'd like to come out this holiday on his own. He arrived this morning and I met him at the airport as usual. He seemed tense and preoccupied, and explained that it had been a hard term at school, and that Bill's death so soon after Kate's had left him very low.

Now we sat on the terrace, in the warm night air, both sunk deep into comfortable armchairs. My eyes began to close as I sipped my third gin and tonic, and I could see that his were closing too. He was however, I saw, looking at me intently through his half closed lids. I yawned widely, I had been up since very early to get ready for his visit and meet his flight, then we'd had wine with a late lunch which always makes me sleepy. He stifled a half yawn himself and smiled at me. "Feeling tired, are you?" he asked. "Heavy limbed perhaps?" I nodded silently in reply, sinking further down in the chair, and putting my drink on the floor. His breathing became heavier and he too sunk lower in his chair, pouring himself a fourth drink from the bottles he had brought out to the terrace with him. He raised his glass to me. "Cheers, Ruth. Going to change your will, were you? Cut me out and give it all to the girls, eh?"

"Only if I die," I mumbled, stunned by his remark and tone.

"Oh, you're going to die alright. Just as Bill did."

Shock hit me, but lethargy kept me sitting, almost asleep in my chair. "What do you mean, just like Bill?" I muttered.

He seemed to sink even deeper down and answered me slowly and somewhat disjointedly. "Bill . . . . well, he had it all, didn't he ..... lots of money . . . . .. prettiest sister."

I almost jerked awake. "No, I'm not, Kate was just as pretty as me, anyway I wanted Bill, I wouldn't have married you even if he'd chosen Kate." I sank back down and repeated more slowly and sleepily, "What do you mean, just like Bill?" His voice came to me once more, slow, jerky, disjointed, but with a note of triumph in it.

"I was with him ..... on the platform ..... pushed him, didn't I." For a moment his eyes closed and he looked half asleep, drugged. In the silence the night sounds were loud and clear. The call of "Mulo. Arre, arrrreee," from across the valley, as Paco returned home from his vineyard. The call of a grouse from close at hand, the rattle of a motorbike as it passed on a nearby road. Then he spoke again, sleepily but confident. I listened in horror as he went on. "It was no accident .... met him after school, didn't I .... wanted a bit for myself ..... but he wouldn't lend me anything said I should live on my salary . . . . .. rich bugger .... all this .... and anything for the girls .... but not me."

"So," I spoke softly and slowly, coming to terms with it. "You pushed him in front of a tube train. Why? That didn't get you anywhere, did it?"

"S'right, pushed him .... sure it did ..... or will," his voice was becoming fainter and slower as sleep overtook him. "Cos, you haven't ..... you haven't changed your will yet, have you? And it all comes to me .... now that Kate's gone. Put something in your drink, didn't I ..... not a biology teacher . . . . .. not a biology teacher for nothing, am I."

He struggled to sit up and open his eyes, fighting his sleep. He smiled then as he looked across at my recumbent figure opposite him. When he spoke again, his voice was firmer, louder, more coherent. "It's something I made up in the lab, you'll just go to sleep and not wake up, nobody will suspect anything. It'll look like a heart attack. Brought on by the events of the last year or so, Kate's and Bill's death, having to cope with his business, that sort of thing." He stopped speaking and his eyes closed again, a snore came from his lips.

I pulled myself together and stood up. "Roger," I half shouted to wake him. His eyes came half open and he stared at me standing over him, in a dazed puzzled way. "Roger, before you nod off, you ought to know something. I saw you put something in the glass. I didn't know what it was, but noted you had given it to me. I switched glasses when you were looking at the picture. Whatever you planned for me, well now you have it yourself. No trace, no suspicion, you said, look like a heart attack. Overwork at school, grief over Kate and Bill I expect, something like that."

28

He was staring at me open mouthed in horror, then his eyes closed and he slipped into a deep dreamless sleep. It won't bring Bill back of course, but at least he won't be able to cheat his own daughters when I'm dead. That won't be long now, as I've got cancer, which is why I get so tired of an evening. It's obviously a family weakness. So when I die, they'll get it all between them, just as we planned.

THE PENANCE OF THE MAIDEN AUNT

Miss Shilitoe was a formidable old lady, there was no doubt about that. At almost eighty she was still a fine looking woman, her face unlined, her figure firm and well proportioned, and it was obvious that in her youth she had been quite a beauty. When she was, as today, in her English mode, dressed in a severe black suit and jacket, a white lace blouse and wide brimmed hat to keep off the sun, she looked the picture of an English spinster. Almost a caricature.

Her nephew Charles, anxious and sweating in the hot Andalucían sun, knew that whilst that was so, there was also another side to her character. She had lived for nearly sixty years, since 1922, in Churriana, a suburb to the north of Málaga, one of her claims to fame being that she had been an acquaintance of Gerald Brennan. This other side of her character took her from being, on the surface, a respectable English maiden lady, to that of a more flamboyant Spanish señorita of advanced years. Her time in Churriana had given her almost fluent Spanish and a seemingly endless number of friends and acquaintances amongst the locals. When mixing with them she joined in their lives to the full and became vibrant and animated.

Charles, who was very fond of her and visited her regularly, had witnessed this change of character many times. Today, just when he needed her to be relaxed and approachable, she appeared to be in her least amenable mood. When she was like this he knew she could wither even the strongest with her straight laced impregnable respectability.

She was a Quaker, or so she claimed, but he knew that if she was, she was surely an unorthodox one. On the other hand, he admitted, he knew little or nothing about the Society of Friends, and they may all have been like her, but he doubted it. When in her Spanish persona she worshipped in the local Catholic church and was on friendly terms with the priest, as she was with others in the area including the Bishop. One day Charles had witnessed her turn on and verbally demolish an official of one of the English Free Churches in the vicinity, by her scorn and a few withering words. The man was some sort of sidesman, or churchwarden or lay pastor, he was not sure exactly what as his knowledge of Free Church terms was even less than that of the Quakers. Charles himself was a staunch Anglican. He knew his aunt didn't like the man, who was a short, tubby, red faced, fussy individual. She considered him to be insincere, condescending and a bore. "Besides which, he dresses in a black cassock, as if he were the Minister," she always said by way of a final assassination of his character. That day the man had overheard her telling some of the congregation how she often went to the local Catholic church in her village to celebrate Mass. "Miss Shilitoe," he had butted in stentoriously. "Don't tell me you go to Popish services, you a Quaker, or so you claim ." All round them a silence had fallen over the worshippers who were leaving the church. The Minister had stood appalled but unsure of how to intervene and Charles had felt discomforted. His aunt had not been at all put out, she had turned to the man and said icily, "I don't recall telling YOU anything. I WAS having a private conversation. If you make a habit of eavesdropping then you must expect to hear much you do not like. I should say that most people here would share few, if any, of your views. As to

31

Popery, I prefer their open fellowship to your bigotry anyday. Come, Charles."

And with that she had left followed by her nephew, to whom the Minister had winked and raised a thumb. Her adversary had stood red faced, to the amusement of those around him.

This morning also, as she and Charles sat sipping pre-lunch sherries in the bar in Churriana, she was very much in her English maiden aunt role, he thought glumly. And he had an urgent and delicate, almost desperate, matter to raise with her. How exactly could he go about it without raising her ire, he pondered miserably.

"Let me bring you up to speed on our plans for tomorrow ...."

The voice of a young Englishman at the next table brought a frown to his aunt's face.

"What is that young man talking about? Why do the young not use language correctly?" she said acidly, in a voice that carried to the man, who stopped talking and glared at her.

Charles coloured and stuttered out a reply sotto voce. "It's a sort of, er, Americanism, I suppose. It means, er, to, er, bring you up to date ....."

"I know what it means, I object to debasement of the English tongue." Again she spoke icily and clearly.

"What's with you, you old biddy." The man, long haired and tattooed, had risen and stood over her. She looked back at him calmly. Behind the man a huge Spaniard, of about fifty, had also got up from his seat and sauntered nearer.

"I believe you heard young man. You have a perfectly good language to use, why do you have to debase it so?" She was polite but adamant.

"I'll give you debase . . . . ," he began, to be interrupted by a stream of Spanish from the large man at his shoulder. Miss Shilitoe answered, just as rapidly, in the same tongue, then smiling slightly said to the young man, "Manolito here asks if I need his assistance, but I have assured him that we are simply chatting. That is so, is it not?"

As she spoke the Englishman turned and saw the large burly figure standing behind him. She went on, "Manolito means little Manolo, you can observe that the title little is given in jest."

"Yeah, well, I suppose we are. Just chatting, that is. Come on, let's get out of here." And with that he and his companion left the bar. Manolito, the fifth of her lovers who she had given up, reluctantly, several years ago because of their age disparity, sat down again with a grin.

Miss Shilitoe turned back to her nephew with a sigh. She was extremely fond of Charles, her youngest sister's son, and he visited her more than any of the others of her family. None of them, she knew, could understand why she lived here, in Andalucia, far from them. He was the only one of them, she believed, who knew of her second Spanish persona. But even he did not know it all, of the lovers she had had over the years. Manolito, who she had broken with almost ten years ago, had probably been the most indulgent on her part. Charles obviously had something on his mind, some worry that he wished to share with her, but couldn't bring himself to speak about it. Perhaps she looked too forbidding. She softened her expression and spoke gently.

"What is it, Charles? Why are you looking so pensive?" When he didn't answer, she finished her sherry, rose and led the way into the restaurant. "Come, you can tell me over lunch."

Everyone in the place seemed to know her and it was ages before the waiters had finished fussing around them, and they were left alone with their soup.

"Now, out with it, what's the problem?" she commanded. At last he managed to speak, the sherry and wine they were now drinking and his aunt's subtly changed manner, loosening his tongue. á "I've met this girl. Well, I met her several months ago during a previous visit to you. She lives in Cártama. Her names's Elena. We're in love with each other."

The sentences came out in short bursts with long gaps in between, but she didn't interrupt. Over the second course he went on more easily.

"This visit, some time after I returned, just a few days ago, I sensed something was wrong. At first it was fine, as it always had been, and then one day she seemed worried and more reserved. I can't get her to say what it is and my Spanish isn't good enough to prize out the reason. I'm not fluent enough. Could you help me, Aunt? Try to find out what the problem is?"

She concentrated on eating, considering, and then said, "I would like to meet your Elena. Could you possibly arrange it for tomorrow?"

The following morning when they set out in Charles' car to drive the short distance to Cártama, she had changed from an English spinster to a Spanish señorita by subtly altering her appearance. Wearing a simple black dress, with her grey hair pulled back and held by a red comb, it was perhaps more her bearing that made the real difference.

She took to Elena at once. The Spanish woman was about two years younger than Charles, had black hair and bright flashing eyes.

34

Soon the two of them were chatting animatedly as she drew out the younger woman's background. Second youngest of a large family, a pharmaceutical chemist with good prospects, she thought her an ideal match for her nephew. She both sang and danced the flamenco, and obviously loved her region and home. There was however, as Charles had said, a certain reserve and worry which clouded her eyes from time to time and raised a barrier between them, when she appeared to withdraw into herself and fall silent.

After a while she sent Charles away, telling him that she wanted to talk to Elena alone. When he had gone, albeit reluctantly, she came straight to the point. She may have been in her Spanish persona, but she was still a formidable commanding old lady. Perhaps even more so than in her English mode to Elena, who was reminded of her late autocratic grandmother.

"Now, tell me, what troubles you, child?" Miss Shilitoe demanded rather than asked. "You can trust me utterly, nothing you tell me will go any further, or shock me, no matter what it is. My nephew tells me that he loves you deeply and I will do anything, and I mean anything, to aid his happiness. He has always shown me love and devotion, far more than any other of my relatives, who I see little of. And I feel drawn to you too, so out with it."

The tale took some extracting but at last, bit by bit, Elena told the old lady everything. It was quite simple, but devastating in its potential. Elena's younger brother had fallen in with a crowd of his contemporaries who experimented with soft drugs. Then one day a pusher had sold them some heroin and crack cocaine. One of the group had become seriously ill, and ended up in hospital. She, Elena, had heard stories of others who had been addicted to such drugs and ruined their lives, some of them even dying. She had become sick with worry for her younger brother and had approached the man and tried to warn him off. He had turned violent and in defending herself she had killed him and, in panic, hidden the body. She had stabbed him with a sharp knife she had taken along to the meeting for protection. She told Miss Shilitoe that the idea of killing him, if he didn't agree to stop dealing with the locals her brother mixed with, had been in the back of her mind all the time. She had felt strongly and now wasn't in the least sorry for what she had done. The trouble was that the Guardia had found the body and worked out the time of his death. One of the sergeants suspected her and if he could find enough evidence, which he might at any time, she would be arrested and imprisoned. She would not involve Charles in any of the mess.

Miss Shilitoe thought for a few minutes after she had heard Elena's story and then said, "What a strange coincidence," a remark that mystified the other woman. Then she went on.

"What I am about to tell you now must go no further, not even to my nephew. As I honour your confidence, so you too must honour mine. During my life in Spain I have had several lovers. The first three I gave up for certain reasons, not important here, and the fifth was sheer indulgence on my part. In the end I had to let him go, against his wishes, as I considered it not fair for a forty year old man to be saddled with a seventy year old woman as I was then. I did so reluctantly for he was, and remains for that matter, a fine man and we are still very good friends."

Elena looked at the somewhat prim figure in amazement. "Incredible, you are truly formidable," she gasped.

"Yes, well, be that as it may, but now to the fourth man, who concerns us here," the old lady continued. "He above all the others was my true love. Or so I thought. Then one day I discovered he was a dealer in hard drugs. I won't bore you with all the details, but I've always detested such people, I've seen too many of their victims. So despite my strong Quaker views on violence, I killed him. I have done my penance in many ways since then to atone, but unlike you faced no human judgement, for no one ever discovered his body, or knew what had happened to him. He simply mysteriously disappeared."

"Thank you for your confidence in me," Elena replied. "It is, as you said, an amazing coincidence. I am sure we both did the correct thing. May I call you tía? For you are like an aunt to me as well as to Charles."

"Of course, and I will call you sobrina in turn, for if I am to be your aunt then you must become my niece. But I had a reason for telling you my story, not just to show that we both had faced the same issue, and resolved it in the same way. Tell me when the man died, and I will say that you were visiting Charles and I at the time, and couldn't possibly have done the deed, I know he will agree to collaborate with us in this. If the sergeant should come to you, refer him to me. Now, you must come to Churriana with us and confess to our priest. He is a good man and will give you a suitable penance and will hold to his vows of secrecy. He is a close friend of mine and will see you at once if I ask it. Then you can set Charles' mind at rest, and in due course you can marry."

When Charles returned they told him a little of their conversation and he agreed at once to say that Elena had been with him and his aunt on the night in question. They didn't tell him of his aunt's crime, but only of Elena's.

Two days later the Guardia sergeant visited them and they gave him Elena's alibi. He wasn't fully convinced but when he approached the local alcalde, who had been one of Miss Shilitoe's lovers, he assured him of her probity. The mayor also sent him to the Bishop who affirmed that she was a reliable witness, and a personal friend. With that the sergeant had to be satisfied, and accept that Elena could not have carried out the crime.

Miss Shilitoe then spoke with her friend the priest and confessed her knowledge of the affair. He looked at her with a wan smile. "I doubt you seek absolution from me. But rest assured, Elena has her penance. Part of it, which affects you, is that she is to keep away from that nephew of yours for a month. Such a test will only surely confirm their love. As to the man who you have both told me of, I confess that I cannot hold his death as being in any way regrettable. I may be wrong, for I know that all life is sacred, but his sort bring misery and death in their wake."

"I tend to agree with you," Miss Shilitoe said. "As you are aware, I belong to a society that renounces violence, but then as you also know only too well the flesh is weak. And no, I ask for no absolution from you, I confer my own strictures for my part in the affair, as I always do. I need no priest to stand between me and my God, not even a good friend like you, and surely I am harder on myself than you would be."

She then took her nephew aside and said, "Charles, the priest has given Elena her penance, and part of it is that she may not see you for a month. That is not a long time to wait, if you love her, so be patient. Now you must do your part, for your share in committing perjury. Let me tell you something. In the past I have had several lovers. Don't look so shocked. I have always made my own atonement for the sins. The first three were also desired by friends of mine, whom I judged in each case to love them more than me, but who unlike me had withheld their favours. I also knew that they would marry them, which I wouldn't, for I have never wished to be in a situation where I was subservient to anyone. I gave each of them up, as penance for my sin, and blessed the unions when they occurred. All of them are now my good friends, both husbands and wives alike. You too, Charles, must do your own penance in this case. When you marry Elena, where do you intend to live?"

"Why, aunt, I will take her back to England. I have my job and life there. But what has that to do with it?"

"No, Charles. She is pure Spanish. A child of Andalucía," his aunt said, ignoring his question. "She would die in England, she needs the sun, the fiestas, the flamenco. Believe me, I know, for I too could not live without them, English that I am. In her case it is even more so. Your atonement is that you must make a life here, with her. Take this month, whilst you wait for her, to learn the language better and find a job. I will be able to help you do that, for I have plenty of friends and one of them at least will offer you a post. In this way you will both be happy, and forget the violence that almost tore you apart."

He looked at her and nodded agreement, he was aware that she was right in her assessment of Elena. He also knew, deep down, that he too loved this country and its people, and that it was not only his attachment to his aunt that had brought him back time and time again.

"Yes, you are right, I will do as you order," he said, then continued. "And you, aunt, what is your penance for your own complicity in the affair?"

Today she was back in the dress and with the air of her English persona. His prim and fearsome maiden aunt. She looked at him with a wry smile.

"I shall give up my latest lover."

She was truly a formidable old lady.

CONSEQUENCES

There was no need for Harry to have gone into Nerja shopping that morning at all. But then if he hadn't, he would never have bought the doughnuts. And if he'd not got a pack of six, his wife wouldn't have said, "Harry, we can't eat three with our morning coffee!" and invited Jenny in from next door, to make it just two each. Whilst they were all having their snack, Rollo phoned Jenny to say he was coming home early, from his job teaching English as a foreign language in the Escuela de Idiomas in Torrox, because he had a cold. He had been teaching in the language school for over a year now, and this was the first time he'd ever come home early. If Jenny had been at home, instead of drinking coffee, eating doughnuts and chatting with Harry and his wife, then Rollo would have just driven straight home, about a ten minute journey. When he discovered she was out, he felt so sorry for himself, and not wanting to go back to an empty house, that he decided to go to the bar next to the school and have a couple of brandies to ease his symptoms. So instead of being home in under a quarter of an hour, because he met Paquito, a friend from Nerja, in the bar, he didn't get back for over an hour with six brandies inside him.

Because Jenny was in Harry's and missed his call, she wasn't expecting him home until six in the evening, for he always stayed in Torrox for his lunch which he ate with the other tutors in the same bar he had gone to for his brandies. If Jenny hadn't been out when he rang, she would have been able to phone Pepe on his mobile and stop him coming to see her. As it was, she had to make her excuses to Harry and his wife when she noticed the time, and rush back to be there to let him in.

Jenny worked two mornings a week in the same language school in Torrox as Rollo, where she was the typist. This suited both of them, as she would go with him in the car and have lunch with him, and then visit the supermarket in the afternoon to get any shopping they wanted and then, in the summer, go on to the beach until he had finished teaching. In the cooler weather she would either sit in the common room of the school and chat to the students and other lecturers, or go and visit friends in the pueblo.

It was during one of these afternoons spent on the beach that she had met Pepe, who worked in a bar restaurant in Torre del Mar, where he did the breakfast and evening meal slots, leaving him free from eleven in the morning until seven in the evening She was an attractive blonde and caught his eye at once when he spied her in a brief bikini, reading and sunbathing. There are few ash blonde Spanish women, and he was smitten at once by the contrast to his usual girlfriends. He was brown, brawny, black haired and full of vital energy, just the opposite to Rollo, who was fair, running to fat and languid. He came as a breath, no a gale, of fresh air, and vanquished the growing boredom of her life.

Soon the only friend she visited on her two afternoons in Torrox was Pepe, who had a flat quite near the Escuela de Idiomas. Two more afternoons, Pepe would drive from Torre del Mar, past his flat in Torrox and on to Nerja, where he would visit her. This arrangement had been in operation for over three months now without any problems. When he came to Jenny's house, he walked along a path to the rear of the row of houses where she and Harry and several other English families lived. Because of the layout of the site and the style of the buildings, he could come to her back door unobserved.

Jenny got back just in time to let Pepe into her house. She was hot and flushed from having to rush back after frantically trying to get away from Harry and his wife, who were both gossips. She had just narrowly missed having to be rude, to manage to get back in time. In the end, Harry's wife had said to him, "Let her go, Harry, she's obviously keen to get away. She's probably got a lover back there. I should be so lucky, stuck with you. It's all these cakes you keep buying, I've put on so much weight I wouldn't attract anyone."

Jenny had flushed red at the remark, even though she knew Harry's wife was only joking. Or at least she thought so.

Because she was so het up, with the rushing and the joke, and to tell the truth a bit full from the two doughnuts which Harry had bought, Pepe and Jenny sat and talked for a bit so that she could recover, before going up to the bedroom. Normally they wouldn't have waited, but rushed straight upstairs the moment he arrived. For this reason they were still in bed when Rollo let himself into the house. If they had been finished and downstairs where they usually had a cup of tea afterwards, Pepe having discovered he liked this strange English beverage, they would have seen him and Pepe could have slipped out. With no harm done. As it was Rollo came in quickly and they didn't hear him. He thought the house was empty, his wife presumably still out somewhere. Feeling even sorrier for himself, and quite woozy from the drink, he went upstairs and into the bedroom.

When he saw them, naked on the bed in the act of coupling, he went beserk and, picking up a brass candlestick, brought it down first on to Pepe's head and then Jenny's. This violence sobered him and seeing he had killed them both, he went back downstairs and phoned the police.

There was no need for Harry to have gone into Nerja shopping that morning. But then if he hadn't he would never have bought the doughnuts. And if he'd not got a pack of six .... none of this would have happened.

Shopping can be a dangerous pastime.

EASY MONEY

In the mirror behind the counter George could see the entrance to the bar. He could also see his own reflection and he quickly checked his appearance. Distinguished, clean shaven, expensive business suit, conservative tie, everything as it should be. On the bar beside him a copy of Sur in English as arranged, this week's copy, not the one in which his advert had appeared. Inserted under Meeting Point, it had read: "Mature, successful business man, too busy to socialise, seeks attractive English speaking lady aged 30 - 50 years for lasting and meaningful relationship. Box No. . . . . .."

Tonight he was meeting the one he had selected from the six replies he had received. Sonia Willmot was 35 years old, a widow, very attractive and very well off. His research consisted of an unobserved scrutiny of her at the hotel where she was staying in Marbella, and a phone call to a private detective in England.

He had given the agent, one he used often, her name and the address in Newcastle she had given him in her letter replying to the advert. His instructions had been a rapid reply, and at low cost. The agent had therefore simply carried out an enquiry by phone. The results were encouraging, her husband had left her very well off on his demise some six months earlier. She was by far the best choice, George had decided, and as his finances were low, he had to move fast.

Sonia came into the bar with her copy of Sur under her arm, but he pretended not to see her, looking down into his drink. She paused and glanced round the room. He was, she decided, the only possible person she was seeking amongst the small crowd of local

Spaniards and casually dressed holiday makers, and he had his copy of Sur beside him.

They got on well together and decided to allow the relationship to evolve by having lunch together the next day. He was never in any doubt, having already picked her out, but she had to be carefully fostered and encouraged. On the other hand speed was also essential, his rent had only a few weeks to go before he would be homeless and his cash was running out. His last two unsuccessful sorties had left him almost penniless. This time he must succeed.

Over the next few days they met for lunch and dinner, and went on outings to Selwo safari park and Ronda. He described to her how he made his living. He told her that he bought and sold shares and currency, and made prudent investments with the profits. She in turn told him of the death of her husband, and of being in receipt of a large sum of money from the sale of his assets. He carefully made no early moves.

It was Sonia who, hesitantly, made the approach however. "George, don't think me presumptuous, but could you help me, if you would, to invest some of it? If it's not improper to ask?"

Elated, he pretended to think for a few moments. "Well," he paused. "I'm putting a twenty thousand pound package together, that's about thirty thousand euros, with my agent on Friday. I could get about 10% interest, all being well. Is that the sort of thing you want?"

"Oh yes, that sounds fine, but how would I go about it?"

He arranged a meeting for her with his agent, Bruno, the next day. Bruno came down from Madrid the following morning on the train. George used him for this sort of deal, for a fee of 10%. This time it would be more as Bruno would also have to loan him the twenty thousand for a day or two. When Sonia told Bruno that she wanted to invest one hundred thousand pounds, he agreed to only charge George 1% on the loan.

There would be no problem with the money. She had an account with Barclays, whose branch in Marbella were only too pleased to transfer the money from her Newcastle branch and make it available in euros.

Bruno explained he would need it in cash, in two days time. She arranged to have it delivered to her hotel. George was with her as a messenger arrived with a small parcel and watched her deposit it in the hotel safe.

She was no fool however and was obviously worried about handing out such a large sum to anyone, despite Bruno's solid appearance and impressive paperwork. This was what George paid him for, to give confidence to the deal. George now played his master card, it never failed.

"Look Sonia, I can't be here to meet Bruno, I have to go off on business for a few days. Could I leave my money with you, and you see to it for me?"

So George put his twenty thousand pounds in her hotel safe, beside her own package. On the morning of the meeting Bruno arrived at the hotel at half past ten as they had agreed, to take charge of the money and give Sonia the worthless documents in return. He phoned George shortly after to report.

"What do you mean, she's checked out earlier this morning?" George shouted into the phone, breaking out into a sweat. "Where's the money? You can't be serious."

He rang off in a panic. He had no money, no flat after next Tuesday and he owed Bruno twenty thousand pounds, plus interest, plus his expenses for his trip from Madrid. He had to run and run quickly, before Bruno brought in his heavies. What had gone wrong, he thought despairingly, as he packed in a hurry.

Sitting on the plane to Gatwick Polly King, alias Sonia Willmot, thought, "How gullible can some people be?" For the cost of a four week holiday on the Costa del Sol, a bit of research in England to find a suitable person to imitate, and the cost of having a parcel full of newspaper (the same Sur in English that had carried the advert, a nice touch that, she thought) delivered to her hotel by a courier, she had made twenty thousand pounds. She hoped George and Bruno could afford it.

SPRINGBOARD

They say that in times of greatest danger, during life threatening events, your past life runs through your mind in a very few seconds. Certainly the circumstances leading up to Neil's ungainly plunge into the pool flashed in front of Petra's eyes as she ran to the side and dived in after him. Or at least that's what she claimed later. Not that she was in any danger, but by the way he had dropped into the water, she knew that he certainly was.

She had been enjoying a late afternoon's sunbathing, after a morning shopping with Neil in Málaga, which had become a habit during their stay in the villa. He, also as usual, had decided to have a dip in the pool. Through half closed eyes she'd watched him come out of their patio doors and saunter to the side, dip a toe in the water, and then go back a few steps and ready himself to dive in. Before he could run to the edge she had sat up and called out, "Do you think you should swim today, Neil? I don't think you're quite sober." When they had finished their shopping, they had met up with a few of their friends and spent a couple of hours in a bar, drinking and eating tapas. To her knowledge, and she hadn't been closely watching him or counting, he had sunk two gin and tonics and several glasses of wine. And a gin and tonic here was about a triple in English measures. As she had known he would, he'd turned to her and almost sneered, "Don't fuss, Petra," before facing the pool once more and diving in.

That first dive off the side had been almost perfect, as if to refute her claim of his being not fully in charge of his faculties. She followed him with her eyes as he swam up and down the pool. He certainly was in good shape for someone well over forty five, she thought, watching his lean brown body cleave through the water. Standing up, she'd glanced casually around the small garden, which was nearly all taken up with the terrace and pool, enclosed by a wall which made it almost fully secluded. The area was only overlooked by the villas on either side, and only by them if their occupants sat at the very edge of their terraces and looked through the patterned concrete blocks set on top of the metre high dividing walls. She and Neil could only look into their neighbours' gardens by similarly going to the extreme sides of their patio.

Looking to her left she had seen that the two young Spanish women staying next door, as usual when Neil was giving his regular late afternoon performance, were watching him. She could never decide if they were attracted or amused by his antics, but whatever it was, they almost always managed to be on the corner of their terrace at this time of day, when he was in the water. Today they were there as normal, she noted with satisfaction.

Half turning to her right she'd noted, again with pleasure, that Mr Turner, who owned the villa on that side had also, as he usually did, found a reason to be on the edge of his property peering through. She had no doubt why he habitually came to stare into their garden at this time of day, as when Neil was swimming she always sunbathed topless, wearing only the skimpiest briefs.

Neil did not seem to mind that their neighbours on both sides regularly spied on their afternoon ritual, in fact he positively appeared to welcome their attention. No doubt he enjoyed showing off to the women and got vicarious pleasure from old Turner drooling over her. It was probably a case of "You can look all you like, but don't touch", she decided. She'd turned to one side and the other, moving her breasts up and down, just to keep his attention, before once more lying on the sunlounger.

She'd watched as Neil had come out of the water and gone to the deep end where the springboard was. As usual he'd gone back to the edge of the tiled area to get a run then sprinted forward on to the board. His trick was to run up the plank, give a skip, bounce on the end and flip high into the air, jack knife and cleave cleanly into the water.

Today, halfway along the board he'd slipped, fallen awkwardly and struck his head on the corner of the plank before dropping into the pool with a loud cry and splash.

The shouts of her three neighbours had mingled with her own as she'd jumped up and ran to the pool, diving in after him It was during this brief period that all the events leading up to the incident had flashed through her mind. Or so she'd said afterwards. But perhaps it was just that she'd been going over and over their life together of late and it only seemed that way. Whatever the truth, she was convinced they had.

She had first met Neil when she was twenty one and working for a firm of architects in Darlington. He owned a building firm and had come into the office to discuss a tender his firm had submitted. He was nearly forty and divorced, and had been smitten by her as soon as he saw her. She had left school at eighteen with few qualifications, with only GCE's in Maths and English. She was good at shorthand and typing, which the school taught, and could work a computer. She got a job in the typing pool of the architects and soon became their senior clerical assistant. "Well, the other two are useless," she told her parents, when she was promoted. One day when she had been with the firm for about a year, the senior

51

partner called her into his office. His PA, a women of about fifty, had had an accident on her way to work in her car and was in hospital. He asked Petra to fill in for her until he knew what would happen. In the event, his PA did not come back to work, but decided to retire to take things easier. Petra had done so well in the job that she was offered it permanently So there she was with a top job and no qualifications.

It was about two years later that she met Neil and, despite their age difference, they struck up a relationship and eventually married. He owned two houses, one in Darlington and one in Hawes, in the Pennines, "for the weekends" as he put it, as well as the villa in Spain. He was, in Petra's words, 'stinking rich' and for about six months she was happy and thought herself very lucky. She had her job, which she loved, had left her grotty flat in Stockton, and was living in the lap of luxury with a partner she loved and whom she thought loved her. Neil was in very good shape and she told her parents that everything was 'tickety boo', as her grandma used to say.

Then one day Neil came home, just after she had arrived back from work herself, and told her that she had to give up her job and stay at home full time, to "make the place a decent home" as he put it. She had laughed and told him that she was happy as things were, and that she didn't want to give up work yet and that she thought they had a good home already. She told him she'd think about it in a year or so, if they wanted to start a family.

"It all came back to me as I ran to the pool, dived in and swam up to him. He was floating, face down in the water, with a crimson stain of blood from the cut on his head spreading on the surface beside it," she said to Madge much later, when they were discussing the affair. Madge was her only confidant in those days as Neil had made her give up her friends one by one over the years. Neil of course did not even know she knew Madge, never mind had made a friend of her.

"Well, when I laughed and told him I didn't want to give up my job," she continued to Madge. "He hit me, hard, in the solar plexus. Drove all the air from my body and made me retch. Then he just walked out of the house. He came back after about an hour and calmly told me that there was more of that if I didn't do as he said. I was terrified. I handed in my notice the next day.

"Over the next three years I led a dog's life. He was a wife beater, but subtle with it. He never hit me where it would show, so I had no black eyes or bruises to explain away, and he used psychological pressure as well. He broke my spirit and I lost all confidence. I'd no one to turn to as I'd no friends left and my parents both thought the world of him, and that I was more than lucky. They wouldn't hear a word against him, and in any case had retired to Wales, and I seldom saw them and never without him. I thought of going to a shelter for battered wives, but felt a fraud, being so well off, for he never stinted with money, and I had no bruises to show. In the end I steeled myself and told him I wanted a divorce. I expected him to flare up and braced myself for an onslaught.

"He just laughed and told me about you."

He had told Petra that his previous wife, Madge, had divorced him, and boasted that she hadn't got a penny out of him. He said that he had had a good lawyer and that he'd paid someone to say that Madge had been having an affair for years, and had then run out on him. He told her that he'd do the same with her and she would be penniless. That was when she'd hunted out Madge and gone to see her. Madge had confirmed the story, adding that the judge had ruled that he had been the innocent party, and told her that she had acted disgracefully. Then she had described how one of Neil's foremen had stood up for her and helped her out, and eventually married her. Neil had sacked the man and had tried to ensure that he never got a job again. However, she had continued, one of Neil's rivals, who didn't like him, had taken her husband on as a Contracts Manager, so in the end he had got a better job.

Madge's story had made her think and she'd realised that she'd have to find somewhere to go if she left Neil. She'd need a flat, money to live on and a job. With no qualifications she'd known that wouldn't be easy. But she'd made up her mind and began to salt away some cash from the money Neil gave her. This was how things had stood when they had come away to Spain for their latest holiday. And all this, she claimed, had flashed before her as she dived in and went to his aid.

She surfaced beside his body floating in the pool and slowly pulled it to the side. The two Spanish women were meanwhile climbing over the screen and lowering themselves on to the patio. It was a good four minutes before they managed this and ran across the paving and leaned down to help pull him from the water. Mr Turner was calling over from his garden. "I've rung O61 emergencies and they're sending an ambulance. If you'll unbolt your back gate I'll come round and help. I can't climb this fence, I'm too old." Both the Spaniards spoke English and understood him, so one of them went across to let him in. When he arrived, he turned Neil over on to his stomach and lifted him from the middle to drain water from his lungs. Then he put him on his back and pulled his tongue from his mouth. Kneeling beside him, he started to give mouth to mouth resuscitation. It was now nearly ten minutes since Neil had first gone into the water.

Suddenly the garden filled with people. Two paramedics took over from Mr Turner and two Policia Local started asking questions of her neighbours. Petra turned from the scene and went and sat on a patio chair, and poured herself a whisky from the bottle on the table.

A short time later an officer from the National Police arrived and took over from the local policemen. He had a woman officer with him, and she crossed over to where Petra was sitting, still only wearing bikini bottoms. She took her by the arm and led her indoors away from the busy scene by the pool.

"Come inside. Now go and put some clothes on, then I'll sit with you till the Captain comes in."

She spoke English with an easy manner and a pleasant accent. Despite the fact that the sun was now dropping in the sky, the evening was still hot and so Petra just pulled on a tee shirt. She then made a couple of telephone calls to tell her parents and Madge what had happened. After about half an hour, the police officer entered and had a muttered conversation with his assistant. He then came over to Petra and, with the female officer translating, questioned her.

"We have already spoken to your neighbours," he began. "They have told me what happened, as they saw it clearly. It was obviously an unfortunate accident, however if you are able I would just like to clarify a few points."

"Of course. Can you tell me how Neil is?"

"The doctor is with him now and we will know better in a short time. Now, your husband slipped off the springboard. You can confirm this?"

"Yes, whilst he was running up to dive."

"Your neighbours say you had called out to him not to swim, as you had been drinking at lunchtime."

She nodded a reply.

"How much had he had? Was he drunk?"

"Not drunk, I don't think so. How much? I'm not sure, two gins and a few wines, I believe."

"But you didn't think him sober enough to swim?"

"Water can be dangerous, if you've been drinking."

He considered this and then gave a nod of agreement. He went on. "Your neighbours say you were not swimming, just sunbathing. Then you went to his rescue and pulled him out?"

"Yes. I seldom swim in the afternoon. I pulled him to the side, but couldn't get him from the pool until the others came."

"Hm. But you didn't do anything to start his breathing? Mr Turner did that later when he arrived."

"I don't know how. All I did was try to stop the bleeding from his cut."

"Was it bleeding much?" he asked quite sharply.

"No. No, I think it had stopped, or at least nearly."

He nodded and relaxed, concern showing on his face. Before he could speak, the doctor came into the room and spoke rapidly in Spanish to the two officers. The two men went out into the garden and the woman police officer came over to Petra.

"I'm sorry, the doctor had just informed us that your husband is dead. In his opinion, he was already dead when you pulled him out of the pool. They're taking him to the hospital to carry out a post mortem now, but it will only be a formality. Can I get you anything?"

Petra shook her head and poured herself another drink, then phoned her mother and Madge again to give them the latest news. She was quite calm, but could hear the satisfaction in Madge's voice when she said, "At least he won't be able to harm you, or any other woman, again. Look, I'll fly out tomorrow and be with you at the funeral."

The daylight was almost gone when the police captain came back into the room.

"I'm sorry, Mrs Slingsby, Petra, but don't blame yourself, you did all you could. Is there anyone who can come and spend the night with you? Would you like my officer here to stay?"

" "No, thank you," she replied. "The doctor has given me some sleeping pills, so I'll be alright. I just want to be alone. A friend and my mother are flying out tomorrow, so I won't be alone for the funeral."

"I'll come back in the morning with a colleague, when it's light, he'll take a few samples for forensics. You know, the blood on the diving board where your husband hit his head, and so on. Don't worry, it's only routine, all three witnesses gave very clear statements as to what happened, it was clearly an accident. We won't come too early, to give you time to sleep in and recover from the shock."

He smiled at her in sympathy and went back outside. Then at last everyone had gone, and she was left alone.

She sat sipping her drink, recalling the look in Neil's eyes, half dazed from the blow to his head, when she had first reached him in the pool and turned him over. It had been fierce as he tried, even then, to dominate her and force her to keep him afloat. It had turned to first pleading and then terror, as he realised what she was doing. She had calmly pushed his head back under the water and held it there, he was too stunned and weakened from the blow to resist. She had towed him face down, slowly, to the edge, but had still had to wait for the two women to arrive and help her haul him out. She had already known he was dead before Mr Turner began his ministrations.

As the evening turned to night she took several decisions. She would sell this villa, but buy somewhere else nearby, as she had come to love Málaga and the surrounding area. Madge's husband could be given the job of running the business for her, that would really rub salt into Neil's wounds, wherever he was, and she herself could take over the office administration. To be going back to work once more was a pleasant thought. She had all night to sit and plan, for she didn't intend to take any pills to make her sleep, and a tired, pale face would help when she met her mother at the airport, and faced the police captain again. Besides, she had to wait until she was sure her neighbours were all asleep, and that nobody was on the edge of their terraces, looking into her garden.

Then she would crawl out on to the springboard and carefully wash off the grease she had spread there early that morning, before the police came back to examine the blood at its end.

BRYNTOR

The Guardia Civil requested the assistance of the British Consul in Málaga, to help sort out the affairs of an old Scottish woman after her death. She had lived for many years near the remote Alpujarran village of Adrajar and had, as far as anyone knew, no living relatives.

An under consul of many years standing, a good speaker of Spanish, was detailed to go to the village to help them. Because the meeting was to be early in the morning, the official travelled to Adrajar the evening before and stayed overnight in the village Hostal. After a fairly substantial meal he joined a small group of local British residents in the bar. When they learnt why he was in the area, they inundated him with such information they had of her.

"She was well over 90 you know, lived out at Bryntor, that's the name she gave her finca, since before the civil war . . . ."

"Totally alone, never mixed with us, had Spanish friends I've heard. But batty, eccentric, you know, a recluse."

"She was a harmless old biddy though. I met her once, to talk to I mean, not just pass by in the street. She was well educated, quite a character I thought."

They all had their own opinions, which got less and less likely as time passed and drinks were consumed. One thought she might be a relative of the MacTaggart who had lived near Gerald Brennan in Murtas, at Cortijo del Inglés. Another claimed, improbably, that she was a direct descendant of Mary Queen of Scots. By the time the last of them had left, just after midnight, he knew little more about her than when he had arrived. Flora Clunny was a 95 year old

Scotswoman, unmarried, who had lived in the remote finca some 3 km outside the village since about 1932. She was somewhat of a recluse, eccentric, did not mix with the local expats but was on friendly terms with some of the local Spanish.

After they had left, he went across to speak to the few Spaniards still at the bar. These were three middle aged men carrying on an animated conversation, , and an old man sitting quietly beside them.

It was the old man who spoke to him first. "You're here about old Flora, are you?"

Surprised, the official asked, "Do you understand English then?"

"No. But I can pick out the words Flora Clunny and Finca Bryntor and I knew a man from the British Consul was coming to help our great Guardia Sergeant!"

After saying this, the old man lapsed back into silence.

The other three now joined in and told him the same things the British had about her, plus a little bit more.

"She was a good friend of ours."

"She hid many of the comrades who had to live on the hill until the death of the tyrant."

"She helped my elder brother Antonio, son of my father Don Antonio here," said one, pointing to the old man in the corner, who nodded but remained silent.

Soon the conversation widened out.

"Have you been to Adrajar before? No? Then you won't know of the mysteries then."

"It's what you British call a 'Bermuda Triangle'. People disappear." Juan, Antonio's younger son, began the story. "The first was Maria José, the schoolteacher. It was in 1938. She was a hard one. My father here knew her and told me all about her. She was of the falange and denounced many people after the fascists came. Then one day she went for a walk and was never seen again."

"The next was Pablo Romano," cut in a second man. "He was the mayor. He'd had to leave the village at the start of the troubles and only came back after the fascists took control. He had a villager shot for stealing some vegetables from his plot. Everyone was hungry then. He just didn't turn up at the Ayuntamiento one morning after leaving his house, and he too was never seen again."

In all they told of seven disappearances between the first in 1938 until the last in 1970. All Franco supporters, all in their own way tyrants in a village where almost everyone supported the Republican cause.

At last the old man broke his silence. "You're all wrong, the very first was the Italian officer and two Guardia. It was just after they captured the village. My eldest son Antonio, named after me, had run off into the sierras. They didn't capture him until 15 years later. Then they took him to the Valle de los Caídos, and made him help in the building of the mausoleum for that son of a bitch Franco. Antonio was ten years older than Juan here, so he was just a kid then and not involved in the war at all."

"But I remember when they came and told you of his death," Juan said. "And I remember now you telling me of the Italian and the Guardia. They went off into the hills, looking for mushrooms, you said, and never returned. No bodies, no sound of gunshots, no blood. Nothing."

"Still, you're alright," they reassured the official. "It's quite safe today, the last disappearance was years ago."

"And then," began old Antonio, then stopped again. "No. Nothing." He lapsed back into silence as the others looked questioningly at him.

The next morning the consular official drove the few kilometres to the finca which was in a small valley. Here Flora Clunny had lived and worked until her death just a few days ago. She had fruit trees, a vegetable plot, hens, goats, pigs and had obviously been almost self sufficient. The previous night old Antonio had explained that his son Juan and his two daughters had helped her over the last few years when the work had become too much for her alone. "She helped my Antonio, and so we repaid our debt."

Waiting at the finca were the Guardia Sergeant, two of his men, Juan and two other neighbours who had also helped the old lady over the last few years of her life.

"If you could sort out her papers, try to find out about family and so on, we will go round the farm, make an inventory of her goods, stock and the like," the Sergeant said.

In the main room was an old intricately carved desk, full of papers which the official started to sort through. There were many photos, some obviously of her childhood in Scotland with 'Mum' and 'Dad' written on the back. One was a picture of two children labelled 'Me and Donald', and then there was a postcard of a small town with 'Bryntor, Ayrshire' across the front. Also there were quite a few pictures of Flora herself in front of the finca and some of her and a man, with 'Me and Antonio' written on the back. By the likeness this was the elder son of old Antonio, brother of Juan. There were also bills and receipts going back many years, letters and much else besides. It was late in the afternoon before he came across a cardboard box which contained the information he was looking for. Clipped together was a small bundle of papers. There was her birth certificate, passport and Spanish residence card. Below them were the death certificates of her parents and of her brother Donald, killed in action in the second world war. Then came a marriage certificate, in Spanish, issued in Almuñécar in 1941. It was between Flora Clunny and Antonio Roberto García Bravo, presumably the son of old Antonio. Next was a photocopy of a notification to old Antonio informing him of the death of his son Antonio Roberto, "traitor and rebel, in the Valle de los Caidos". Underneath this was a Will, also in Spanish, made in 1980 in Motril. It was the Last will and Testament of Flora Clunny which stated that she had, to her knowledge, no living relatives. She left all her possessions to old Antonio, father of her husband, and if he died before her, to his son Juan, his daughters and their children.

At the bottom of the box was another sheet of paper but before he could read this there was a commotion outside, and the Guardia Sergeant called him. "Señor, come quickly."

He picked up the documents and ran out of the door. The Spaniards were standing around the door of a small stone shed, which had obviously been forcibly opened.

"We couldn't find a key for this, and so we've just broken in," the Sergeant explained.

The official looked inside and saw a line of skeletons, eleven in number with names on cards at their heads and piles of clothes at their feet. He saw that the first three had uniforms below them and that the fourth was headed 'Maria José Conde Byass'.

"What's it all about, Señor?" asked the Sergeant helplessly.

The official read out the marriage certificate and the Will as they stood in the dying daylight in front of the macabre remains. He raised his eyes and saw that old Antonio, silent as ever, had joined them. He then read out, more slowly as it was in English and he had to translate as he went, the last sheet of paper.

"Confession of Flora Clunny. December 10th 1974. I, Flora Clunny, confess to the judicial killing of eleven fascist terrorists. Ten by poison that I distilled myself from oleander and gave to them in wine. The other by stabbing. No one else was inolved or is guilty of these deaths." Then were listed   eleven names, nine men and two women."

He raised his eyes again and once more looked at old Antonio.

"Did you know of this?"

"Yes, Señor," replied the new owner of the finca.

"And the eleventh too? Is that what you started to say last night?"

"Oh yes. She once lived in the village, but had moved to Almuñécar by the time of the wedding. She saw Antonio after the ceremony and he, not Flora, my dear daughter-in—law, stabbed her. Fortunately it was late at night and the street was deserted. He had to kill her to silence her, she was probably the worst of the lot and would have denounced him. We brought her back here and put her with the others. Oh yes, I was at the wedding, that's when I discovered the truth about the disappearances, and found out what a good comrade she was. The Sergeant was looking more and more perplexed.

"At your convenience, could you two please explain just what you are talking about, and what all this is?"

He waved his hand towards the eleven silent sets of bones.

BANK ROBBERY

The first time he went into the bank in Río de los Olivos, he felt almost affronted. It was a branch of the Cajamontes bank, with only room for two staff behind the wooden counter, despite the fact that Río was quite a sizeable.town. What he had found almost a slight to him was that there was no security at all. Leaning over the counter he could see an open drawer, almost within his reach, full of banknotes. He had come into the bank with the agent from whom he was buying his villa, and when they were outside, their business complete, he commented on this lack of security.

The agent had looked at him and smiled. "They don't need any, do they?" he had said, looking around. The bank was at one side of a small square through which ran the narrow main road, with trees down each side. At either end of the square the road turned a sharp right angle bend, only wide enough to allow traffic to go in one direction. Mirrors were set on the wall to allow oncoming vehicles to see if the road was clear.

"Not a good place for a speedy getaway, is it," he had continued. "And then, think of where the town is, with only the one road on either side."

Río de los Olivos was about an hour's drive from the main road at the bottom of the hill, in the Montes de Malaga. The road was narrow and winding in both directions, passing through two villages to the west before returning to the coast, whilst the road from the east came straight up the hillside to the town.

"Apart from the problem of getting out of the square, by the time anyone got to the bottom of the hill, the Guardia would have more than enough time to seal the ends of the road," the agent had concluded, stating the obvious.

The man had nodded and smiled back. "Better than grilles, bullet proof glass, alarms and so on," he had agreed. What had disturbed him, and he had found almost an insult, was that for years in England he had made his living from robbing banks and post offices. Well guarded premises, which nevertheless he had managed to rob, without ever being caught. And here, in rural Spain, was a small unguarded bank, as far as he could see full of cash, and apparently unrobbable. It was a slur to his professionalism, a slight to his ego.

Over the following years, living only a few kilometres from Río, he visited the Cajamontes bank in the town many times, and on each visit worried at the problem of how to raid it. It was as if his honour depended on him finding a solution. After just over three years from his first visit to the bank, he thought he had found the answer. Fortunately for him it was also a good time to spend time on his own doing preliminary research. His last partner had just left in a huff and returned to England. He had met a possible replacement in Marbella, but as yet she had not moved in. He was in the meantime living alone and so had plenty of time to make his plans.

Some way down the road from the town to the east a dirt track branched off and ran for about twelve kilometres to another town, San Marcos, just before joining the main road to Ronda. This track was no good in itself as an   escape route, as it would take even longer to drive down than the two surfaced roads, and would also be sealed at the end by the Guardia. However a short way down, it came to within two kilometres from the main road before veering off again. He put on shorts and boots, drove down the dirt track to where the map showed it closest to the Ronda road, and found a spot to park off the track behind some olive trees. Leaving his car out of sight behind the trees, he set off to walk the short distance between the track and the road.

Near the road he found a dry river bed which he entered and walked down. This led him to the road, out of sight of the traffic passing by on it, to the mouth of a culvert which was nearly two metres in diameter. He went through the culvert, under the road, and continued along the bed of the dry river, still out of sight of vehicles passing on their way to and from Ronda. He soon came to a minor road which he saw on his map would take him to the N340, the busy motorway running the length of the Costa del Sol.

He retraced his steps, recovered his car and drove back up to Río. The following day he went down the hill again, along the road to Ronda and turned off onto the minor road he had reached the previous day, and pulled up next to the spot he had walked to, retracing his steps to the culvert to make absolutely sure. Nearby he found a spot where he could park his car out of sight. His preparations were now complete.

Every month the bank in Río paid out the pensions to all the old and widowed people in the town, and on this day there would obviously be more cash in the drawer than normal. He chose the next pension day for his raid. He was so confident of success that he told his new girlfriend that he would come to Marbella two days later, to pick her up and take her to see his villa. His confidence came from knowing that his planning was meticulate and that in the past he had always been successful. He felt happy, keyed up by the prospect of action, and no longer irritated by the presence of the unguarded bank.

Two days before the planned attack, he drove down the track and parked his car once more behind the grove of olives, and again walked down to the culvert. This time he then climbed up to the road and walked to a nearby layby where buses stopped. Here he caught a bus to Torremolinos, bought a crash helmet with a darkened sun visor and a workman's full length overall. Late in the afternoon he stole a moped which had been left outside a supermarket and rode it out of town. Once out into the countryside he stopped and removed the number plate, which he threw into the ditch. He then rode back to where he had left his car behind the olives, hid the bike in the same place and returned home in his car.

Mario, a goatherd from San Marcos, who tended his flock on the hill above the spot where he had left the moped, had seen both visits the man had made in his car and had gone down to look at it whilst the man was away walking. Mario was used to the strange ways of the foreigners in the area, and had just assumed the man was out for a day's hike. It was after dark when the man exchanged the car for the moped, and so Mario was back home. The next morning he saw that the car, which had still been behind the trees the previous evening when he returned to San Marcos, had now gone and that it had been replaced by the moped. He walked down for a closer look, but didn't tamper with it or tell anyone about it, but thought that he might come out and take it if it stayed there for any length of time. His daughter was getting married in a few months time and he could do with some more money to ensure she had a good send-off. He thought he might be able to sell the moped to a dealer in Fuengirola, even without its papers, but he would need to check first.

The following morning the man rose early, drove down the dirt track to the moped, put on the overalls, gloves and crash helmet, and so disguised drove back up to Río de los Olivos. He pulled up outside the bank just after it had opened and entered it, taking out a handgun. The   robbery went almost too easily. He had practised the Spanish phrases he would need and herded the waiting queue of pensioners to one side, saying, "Poneos al lado," move over to the side. He then pushed a sack over the counter to the two bank employees, the manager and his assistant, and told them to put all the money from their drawers into it, "Pon el dinero en el saco". These phrases, even if not grammatically correct, were understood by the people in the bank.

The bank manager remained calm and told everyone to do just as they were ordered, and calmly filled the bag with money. He knew that the thief would not be able to escape but would be caught at the end of the road.

Telling everyone to stay inside for five minutes, the man ran out of the bank and remounted his scooter. It was then that, for him, two unfortunate things occurred. The first was that coming slowly round the corner was a large lorry that even a moped could not pass. He had to sit and wait for several seconds before he could get round the back of the lorry and drive off down the road. The second was that one of the three local policemen walked into the square during these few crucial seconds of delay. One of the old men in the bank, regardless of the bank manager's instructions, put his head out of the door and shouted to the policeman that the moped rider going round the corner had just robbed the bank. As the man rode off, the policeman pulled out his pistol and fired a couple of shots hopefully after him.

Soon the bank manager was talking to the Guardia and telling them of the robbery.

"It was a foreigner, English, I think, by his accent," he said, and shortly after that the roads were blocked by Guardia patrol cars.

The man felt one bullet hit his thigh as he rode away, causing him to wobble but not come off the moped. He rode off down the road, turned off onto the dirt track and reached his hiding spot behind the olive trees. By the time he got there he had lost quite a lot of blood but put on a rough bandage to stem the flow. The bullet was not in the wound, but had simply passed through his thigh and he thought that he would be alright until he reached his car, in which he had a full first aid kit. It was not the first time he had been shot at during his career, nor indeed the first time he had been wounded, and knew that the policeman had been lucky to hit him at all. He set off walking downhill as fast as he could, leaving the moped, overalls and crash helmet behind. Walking opened the wound up again and he lost more blood, and this together with the hot sun beating down on him made him giddy and lightheaded. At last he stumbled into the culvert and sank down gratefully into the shade to rest for a while.

He was never seen again. After a few days waiting for him in Marbella, his girlfriend gave up and went off with someone else.

His car was found, broken into by a group of teenagers, driven around by them for a short while and then sold on to a group of car thieves and finally sold in Morocco.

His villa stayed empty for years, slowly decaying. People used to say, "I wonder whatever happened to old what's his name? He hasn't been out for years."

The money was never recovered or a cuplrit found, and the Cajamontes bank installed some security screens to stop the bank being robbed again.

Old Mario took and sold the moped and the crash helmet to help pay for his daughter's wedding. When he went to get it, he found the overalls torn in the leg and covered in blood. Several days later he listened to the story of the bank raid and heard that the policeman was boasting that he had hit the robber. Nobody believed him, but Mario wondered. He set off down the hill following the path he had seen the man take. Two days later, after searching the area, he came across his body in the culvert, already part eaten by stray dogs or foxes.

Beside the body was a bag containing over six million pesetas. His daughter had a very fine wedding indeed.

EL CIEGO, THE BLIND ONE

The first thing I noticed as I walked down the steps off the jet standing on the runway was how the hot air hit me. After the cool of the air conditioned plane it was almost like meeting a solid wall, that at least had not changed. Walking across the tarmac I entered the bus that would take me, and the rest of the passengers of the flight, to the arrivals area of the airport. I reflected that that too had not changed over all the years when I had visited my aunt Sasha during my childhood and teens, it had always been the same. What had changed were the smells. In those days, it must be nearly twenty years ago now, the first thing to strike you as you descended the steps was the smell. After the anonymous air of Gatwick or Heathrow, the aroma of Spain appeared to me to be exotic. A mixture of what I took to be perfume from olive trees, stagnant water festering in the heat and cheap cigarettes, but perhaps was something quite other, invaded the nostrils at the same time as the heat struck. Now the air smelled quite different, neutral, just the same as that of Gatwick that I had left just over two and a half hours ago. Perhaps, in reality, nothing had changed except my perceptions. The difference between the impressions of a youngster to that of a more cynical, middle aged .... businessman, was what had really altered.

Shortly after, walking out of the arrivals hall into the blinding June sunshine of Málaga, I saw that I did not recognise anything. The last time I was here, just before my aunt's death, I remember walking across the car park, over a footbridge to the railway station. In front of me now the car park, though different, was still there, but there was no obvious way to the trains across it. I remember my cousin George, Sasha's son, writing that the terminal had all been altered, in one of the few letters he had written after her death. As I had only ever written back once, too busy with the difficulties of setting up my operations in the UK and northern Europe, his too had soon stopped. I didn't even know if he still lived in the same old rambling converted stone farmhouse near Coín, or whether, after his mother's death, he had moved nearer to Málaga. He had told me that he was starting work with the Policia Nacional in the city. As a child born in Spain of a marriage between my aunt, an Englishwoman of Russian descent, and a Moroccan resident in Spain, and speaking English, Spanish, Russian and Arabic fluently, he had had no trouble in finding employment. He was aiming for the detective branch or even, if possible, the Spanish secret service. How the two careers of cousins can go in completely opposite directions, I thought now.

I had no need now of trains though, and walked towards the taxi at the head of the line, waiting for passengers. My operations were now very successful and these days I didn't travel by bus or train anymore. I had mixed feelings about coming back to Spain, especially on business. I had made a rule not to work in America or southern Europe. Too many guns, especially carried by policemen. However this time I had made an exception at the request of an old friend. And the fee was very high.

Thinking of friends, I thought naturally of Ciego. During my childhood, when on holiday in Coín, George (Jorge in Spanish, I remembered), Ciego and I were inseparable. Now business commitments and my personal safety permitting, he was someone I might look up, if I could find him. José Maria, El Ciego. Perhaps I'd better explain, El Ciego, which means the blind one, was his nickname. Well, not his nickname as such, we called people gordo, fatty, or rubio, blondie. But Ciego was different, something we don't have in English, but which is the norm around here. It was his apodo and as such applied to all his family. Virtually all the families had an apodo, some with specific meanings like Ciego, and others just made up words. These replaced surnames, which are complex in Spain, I can't even remember José's surname, if I ever knew it. He wasn't blind of course, his father and grandfather were called Ciego too, and all his brothers, it was the family apodo. Presumably one of his distant relatives had been blind and the name had stuck.

The taxi took me to a small, mid priced hostal, quite near the port. I'd specified this, not because I couldn't afford a pricy hotel, but because when I was working I wanted somewhere small and quiet to stay, unobtrusive, away from the crowds. I put my three cases on the bed and took a selection of objects from each. They had been scattered through my luggage to avoid detection and now I began assembling them into one unit, which I checked to see was undamaged and in working order before dismantling it once again and hiding the various components in different locations in the room.

The next morning I went back to the airport and hired a car, and then drove east along the N340, turning off at Algarrobo Costa and up into the hills to the largish village of Las Yucas. It was an area I didn't know at all, and I spent several hours exploring and making sure I knew the town well. I found a clump of olive trees on the hillside facing the main square which would be ideal for my purpose. I then walked through the square and studied the front of the town hall, where I had been told the dignitaries would gather at the fiesta that weekend.

After a beer and a couple of tapas I drove back past Málaga and up to Coín, turning off towards Cártama just before entering the town. This is where Sasha's villa had been and I drove past it, reliving old memories. José Maria had lived a short distance away down a dusty track. José Maria, I thought, together with the female equivalent Maria José, was a common name in Spain. Joseph and Mary, Mary and Joseph. I had known at least three other José Maria's in Coín alone as a child. Coincidentally the subject of my present visit is also a José Maria. Josí Maria Ramos Sanchez, Mayor of the town Las Yucas, and a well known local businessman, and socialist member of the Junta de Andalucia. His business and political activities have apparently angered my present clients and are causing them financial and judicial problems.

I returned to Coin and stopped at a small bar and bought a coffee. Obliquely, because I didn't want to bring attention to myself, I asked about George (Jorge) and Ciego. One thing that has surprised and pleased me since I have been back in Spain is how the language has come back to me. As a youngster, spending all my holidays at Sasha's and mixing with the village kids, my Spanish became fluent. Even after the gap I seem to be able to speak it quite well. None of the people in the bar however knew anything about either of them, but one old man did remember Sasha and her family. I didn't press them much and left quickly, as I half thought I recognised the old man, Paco he was called, but that's no help as there are numerous Pacos around here, and I was worried he might also have recognised me.

The next three days before the fiesta, which was due to start on Friday evening, I spent scouting the area between Las Yucas and the coast road. I was worried that there were only three possible roads, and all of them narrow and winding. I did however manage to find two or three unsurfaced tracks that I could also use. These would take me away from any road blocks that might be set up.

I had a lot of time to think of course, and a lot of my thoughts turned to the three of us and our childhood together. One memory came back of Ciego. When he was excited, or tense, under stress or the centre of attention, such as when he entered competitions in Coín's fiestas, he had a habit of tugging at his left ear and then sweeping his unruly hair off his forehead. He did this unconsciously and the rest of us would mimic him in merriment much to his embarrassment.

To fill in time before Saturday, I also visited Nerja caves and the castle in Málaga. Walking up to the castle I recalled previous visits with Sasha and George, and how George and I would race round the walls pretending to be Christians and Moors. The days were hot and sunny, as you would expect here in June, and I knew I was becoming too relaxed and nostalgic. It was a good thing I had not found George or Ciego, I realised, or I might have approached them and put the whole mission, and my own safety, in danger. I had to realise, I told myself, that I was now living a different life and had a job to do.

Saturday came at last and I put on shorts and walking boots, and retrieved all the parts of my weapon that I had distributed around the room, putting them in a rucksack together with a bottle of water. I drove once more along the N340 and up the road to Las Yucas. I parked the car about four kilometres away near the start of one of the dirt tracks I had found, and walked the rest of the way to the town.

Then I climbed the hillside to the grove of olives opposite the square and made sure there was no one nearby. It was fiesta and so I hadn't expected anyone to be out in the campo working, but you can't be too careful in my line of work. I had plenty of time as it was only just one and the mayor was not due to leave the town hall until three, according to the programme. I knew that in reality it could be, indeed probably would be, much later than that.

The fiesta had started the previous evening and looking down on the town I could see it had been decorated with flags and streamers, and there were plenty of people in the square, where a temporary bar had been set up. A band was playing in one of the roads leading into the square, where some sort of event had just finished. At two o'clock it quietened down and I took the various pieces out of my rucksack. Quickly I assembled my rifle and fixed the telescopic sight. I checked it was in good order and loaded it. Then I scanned the front of the town hall through the sights. It was so powerful I could see every little detail, I could even read a typed notice pinned to the door. It was now just a matter of waiting.

At about two minutes past three, several rockets were let off from in front of the town hall, and people began to come back into the square. At three fifteen more rockets were let off and presently the doors opened. I looked through the sight after studying once more the photo of José Maria Ramos Sanchez, which in any case I knew quite well by now. With heavy glasses, a beard and a moustache, he was easy to spot. He came to the door and stood on top of the steps, pausing before going down into the crowd.

I focussed the sight on his heart. Just as I was pressing the trigger he raised his left hand and pulled his ear, and was just in the act of brushing his hair back from his forehead when my bullet hit him.

A groan left my lips, it was Ciego. I had killed my childhood friend. I sat numb and stricken. I knew I shouldn't have broken my rule and taken on a contract outside the UK and northern Europe.

Despite the rifle being silenced, the police in the square easily identified where the shot must have come from, and set off at once to run in my direction. It was a good way to come, over 500 metres, and I knew I'd left enough time to get away. It was all a matter of good planning. But instead of moving away I sat still, the gun on the ground beside me, grieving and waiting.

The first policeman on the scene was in plain clothes, running up the hill and motioning the others to spread out and cover him. Without surprise I recognised George, who unlike Ciego hadn't changed at all or taken to glasses and facial hair. It wasn't a surprise, not really. If a prominent local figure, who had received death threats and was pursuing the mafia gangs of the area, needs protection, and he has a friend in the national police in the CID branch, it's only logical that he is put on the case.

As he got nearer, I raised my gun. I had no intention of using it, but I pointed it at him.

"George," I said, tears in my eyes.

He brought his gun up but did not shoot me, as I hoped he would. Instead, he lowered his gun and took the rifle out of my unresisting grip, motioning for the others, the two local police and the two guardia, to stop where they were.

"Primo?" he said in Spanish. "Cousin, is that you? Do you know what you've done? You've just shot José Maria, El Ciego, your friend. It's a good job we insisted he wore a bullet proof vest."

So I'd not killed him. I'd just bruised his ribs and sitting here, awaiting trial, I'm glad. I'll get life of course, as they've connected me to previous jobs I've done.

In fact, I've told them all about them. You see, I just can't live with what I'd become.

Yes, it's me that has become El Ciego. The blind one.

OVER THE EDGE

The narrow road to Las Hojas climbs over 600 metres from the coastal plain to the village, in a continuous sequence of hairpin bends and long straights. To one side of the road the sierra falls away steeply, whilst on the other it rises almost vertically to join the slope above. On the worst bends the cornice road is protected by crash barriers, some of steel posts and rails, and the others of older low stone blocks set intermittently on the roadside. The remainder, that of the straight sections and gentler bends, is unprotected. As the British agent, who sells many of the houses to the growing expatriate community, tells his clients, "It's not the Guardia Civil you need to worry about if you drive over the alcohol limit, it's avoiding driving over the edge!"

William Ambrose was sitting on one of these low stone crash barriers in a small lay-by, several kilometres below Las Hojas. From where he sat he had a good view of the road winding above and below him. When agitated it was his practice to jump into his car and race down the narrow road for some distance, park, and let his mood change before returning home. Looking up, he saw coming down from the village the unmistakeable car belonging to Roger, "Call me Rog," Bray. Bray was the unwitting cause of his agitation, and on seeing the car fear and panic rose up in him. He ran back to his own vehicle and careered off once more down the hill. Such was his panic that he approached an unprotected bend too fast, braked too late and too hard, skidded and shot over the edge. His last conscious thoughts were the words of the estate agent, someone who he had long since fallen out with, and who he was no longer speaking to. Poetic justice indeed.

Shortly after, a horrified Roger Bray stood looking down at the remains of the car, together with several Spaniards, as it burnt out in the barranco below.

The roots of the tragedy went back many years. William Ambrose, always William, never ever Will or Bill, was an ex-teacher of English and R.E. For many years he had taught at a large Midland Comprehensive. Tall, impeccably dressed, sandy haired with a bristling moustache, he was an imposing figure. He was always over polite and punctilious in his language. Never a "who" when it should be "whom", or "I" when "me" was the correct word, he came across as cultured to some but obsessive to others. The slightly manic gleam in his eyes gave a clue as to the reality.

He had as a schoolteacher three failings. He could not keep a class in order, a weakness exploited mercilessly by his pupils. He had an inability to relate to people and so could not get along with his colleagues, causing unrest in the staffroom. His third failing, which was unknown to most others, except the headmaster, was his fascination with the older girls, especially their lingerie. This last was also known to several of the girls, most of whom kept out of his way, but were resigned to seeing him staring at them on the games field.

One of the girls, Betty Williams, well known for her forwardness, deliberately led him on and then accused him of attempted rape. Her father, a burly building labourer, visited the school, caused a scene and struck William on the nose.

Ambrose was lucky in that the event occurred before the days when an accusation of sexual harassment was sure to cause a national scandal, and also that Betty's father had assaulted him. The incident drove Ambrose, not for the first time, over the edge, producing a nervous breakdown, and he was off work for a lengthy period. During this time the headmaster and Betty's father, who were both aware of her character, struck a deal. No prosecution for molesting the girl or for assault on the teacher. The headmaster was then able to have Ambrose retired, at the age of 49, on grounds of ill health.

Fortune once again shone on William, as he sold his house for an enormous profit at the height of the housing boom, bought his place in Las Hojas inland from the Costa del Sol at a low price, invested the profit and lived comfortably off his pension and investment income. No one had cause to complain, except perhaps the tax payer funding his pension and the purchaser of his house, who was soon a victim of negative equity when house prices slumped.

During all this time he had been supported by his wife Ann. She was several years younger than him, fair haired and "county" in both accent and dress. Despite his difficult and unstable character she had been quite happy during their marriage, until the move to Spain. She had not wanted to move abroad, and was unhappy living there, and became much more aware of his peculiarities.

He started writing stories, "Not for publication, just for my own pleasure and reading," he told such friends that they managed to keep in the district. These stories centred on the expat community. Ann would invite them to dinner and from their comments William would evolve their "life stories". Most of these were wildly inaccurate but, for him, became reality. Janet Pusey, a blousy well developed matron, really had been, in his own mind, a prostitute in Leeds. Jerry Paxman, who in real life had been a postman, to William was a crooked County Councillor from Exeter, and so on.

A second obsession, which had started in England but was now much worse and more developed, was his insistence that Ann wear sexy underwear. She wore the silk and the transparent lingerie, the easy to undo front fixing bras, and the crotch opening pants unhappily under her flowery conventional dresses.

Some ten years after they had moved to the village, Roger Bray arrived. Rog was a widowed Eastender, just older than Ann, with a coarse accent. He had been the owner of a small publishing house in Bethnal Green, until he sold it on to his partner just after the death of his wife, and moved to Las Hojas. He had never let on to anyone what his job was, as if he did he was inundated with manuscripts by would-be authors. He retained this practice after his move to Spain, simply saying he "had had a firm in the East End". On a visit to Roger's house William had seen on the desk a replica pistol, a lifelike gun but in reality a cigarette lighter, given to him by his staff when he sold the firm. William however thought it was real and so built up and wrote a story of Roger being the boss of an East End "firm" of gangsters.

He left the story, newly typed, on the table where Ann found it, just prior to a visit by Roger. She quickly put it in a drawer but forgot to tell William.

The next morning, after the visit, he hunted in vain for the story whilst Ann was out in the village, and convinced himself that Roger had found it and taken it away. His unstable nature then took over. To him the story was the reality, the gangster Roger would discover that he, Willliam, knew all about him and come after him. In a high state of alarm and agitation he raced off down the mountain and parked in the lay-by. He saw to his horror that Roger was pursuing him, gun at the ready. This drove him over the edge, both mentally and in reality.

Nine months after the funeral Roger went to Ann's house for dinner. Since being the first on the scene of the accident he had been in close and constant contact with her, feeling some sense of responsibility. Tonight he had some bad news for her. He had told her of his past as a publisher and offered to take away William's collected stories to read, and if suitable send them to his old partner for publication.

"They're no good, I'm afraid, poorly written, and in any case highly libellous. I must say I can't see Mrs Pusey as a call girl myself, but enjoyed reading about my East End gang and moll."

Ann blushed, as she had meant to remove that one before giving them to him.

"But they're no good for publication, I'm sorry."

Ann was not at all concerned. She had discovered that with the investment income and the insurance on William's life, she was in no need of any payment for their publication. She had also become increasingly fond of Roger, finding his easy going nature relaxing after William's punctiliousness. She no longer wished to leave Spain and was now more than happy living in the village. Her voice had become softer, less strident and "county" in its nature.

Tonight for the first time since William's death she was wearing under her sheath dress, itself a change from her usual flowery ones, a set of exotic translucent silk underwear. Roger did not know this, "At least not yet," she thought.

After dinner, on the roof terrace, she brought out two glasses of brandy and bent over to hand Roger his, allowing him to see her breasts, lifted and separated by the bra, through the gap in her low cut dress.

"Shall we have these inside? It's getting midgey out here, and it's very public."

She gazed around the quiet, empty roofs and terraces surrounding them, turned and swayed gently away from him into the house.

"I don't suppose you've ever witnessed a crime? Well, most people haven't, have they?"

My guest paused, waiting for a reply. I remained silent, concentrating on the crossword puzzle which I had half finished. We were sitting on the terrace of my villa in the hills, just above the Andalucian holiday resort of Marbella. I filled in another answer in the puzzle, to the clue: 'Conflict CID started diverted attention (10)', trying not to be, as was the answer 'distracted' by him. My caller was not however to be put off.

"Yesterday, I was sitting outside a bar in Estepona when I noticed a man approaching a woman from behind, as she was walking along the street. He had his hand held out and as he passed her, he hooked the bag off her shoulder and ran off with it." Pausing, he added sugar to the coffee I'd just brought him, and stirred vigorously. "Great, thanks," I replied, filling in 'snatch' to the clue 'Grasp victory at the last moment (6)', the 'a' crossing the one in distracted. "What?" he asked. "What's great about seeing a robbery?" "No, sorry. No, I didn't mean great that you saw . . . . . . what I meant was that you've just helped me fill in a clue." I sipped some more of my drink, smiling at him. "Fill in a clue? What are you talking about? Don't you want to know what I did?" He relaxed back into the cane chair, frowning at me.

I gazed into the distance, not really seeing the brown hillside with its olive groves and white villas, or the distant sea beyond. It was too much, I thought, he had turned up unexpectedly and, as far as I was concerned unwelcome, just after I had settled down with my coffee, to fill in the crossword in today's paper which I had purchased earlier that morning in Marbella.

"Followed," I muttered, half to myself.

"Did you say 'I followed him'? I couldn't quite hear. Well yes, I did. As he ran off I went after him, keeping out of sight as much as I could. In the end he went into another bar some distance away."

As he went on to describe how the thief had met up with an accomplice and how the two of them had rifled through the bag, then how he went back out into the street, found two local policemen, and brought them to the bar, I put 'followed' into the grid. I didn't explain that I'd said 'followed' as I'd deciphered the clue 'Double over short oriental who brought up the rear (8)'. The puzzle was now almost complete, and as I worked out all but the last clue, I listened with half an ear to him describe how he had led the officers up to the two thieves.

My thoughts were diverted from the final clue when he grabbed my arm to claim full attention. He always made sure that he took centre stage in any conversation and allowed no diversions. He pointed to a bruise under his discoloured left eye. "I got that from one of them as they tried to escape," he complained. "And then when we returned to the first bar, the woman was nowhere to be seen. No one seemed to be aware of the incident, which in any case had taken place over half an hour before. I got no thanks from the policemen who seemed reluctant to take any action to find out where she'd gone, and simply took the two robbers away."

He was always moaning, I thought, reading the last clue, and trying to sympathise with him at the same time. "Never mind," I said. "At least you were responsible for their capture. And presumably she would get her bag back when she reported the theft." "But that's not all," he broke in with exasperation. What more, I wondered, concentrating on the final clue, 'Street conflict over animal bedding (5)'.

"As I went into the bar," he continued. "The barman and another local policeman accosted me. I'd not paid for my tapas and drinks when I'd got up to follow the thieves, you see. So he'd called the police. I ended up, not only with a black eye, but also in the same police station as the bag snatchers. It took me over an hour to sort things out, before I was able to explain everything to their satisfaction, pay what I owed and leave."

It was hard not to smile at his story. "What rotten luck," I murmured abstractedly, still working on the clue.

"It's always the same," he moaned. "But to cap it all, when I got back to my car I'd got a parking ticket. It was the final ...."

He broke off, distracted by my stifled chuckle and my muttering to myself.

"What? What are you going on about?" he snapped.

"Straw," I said in satisfaction, filling in the last blanks.

"Yes, I was telling you, it was the final straw." He always has the last word.

Made in the USA
Charleston, SC
28 May 2014